Anaesethetist rather than surgeon . . .

But it was the offer of a job; a job with the mobile accident service which had so caught at her imagination!

Bethany flicked rapidly over to the second sheet attached to the first. This one *was* typed, and it was a contract. It had her name filled in. It also stated a rate of pay which was high enough to make her jaw drop. Goodness, if *that* was what was offered in the private sector . . .

The money wasn't important, a bonus rather than an incentive, even if thinking so made her less practical than she should be. The main point was the job. Bethany turned back to the first page again. The handwriting made it read like a personal invitation.

That was a ridiculous thought; but the bold sharpness of the writing brought a clear picture of raven-black hair, the lean planes of a face, a thin mobile mouth and a tough jaw. And vivid, electric-blue eyes.

He'd probably be a bastard to work for, Bethany's mind told her warningly, even while the blood surged along her veins in a race of triumph.

Barbara Perkins began writing when her children were small as a way of combining her nursing training with an earlier ambition to be a writer. The children are grown up now but Barbara still writes Doctor-Nurse Romances because, she says, hospitals are facinating worlds of their own, and where else would you find all the ingredients of drama under one roof? Modern nursing information comes from friends still in the profession and from a daughter-in-law who is a nurse. Barbara lives near the sea in Kent.

FLIGHT OF SURGEONS

BY

BARBARA PERKINS

MILLS & BOON LIMITED
ETON HOUSE   18-24 PARADISE ROAD
RICHMOND   SURREY   TW9 1SR

*First published in Great Britain 1988
by Mills & Boon Limited*

© Barbara Perkins 1988

*Australian copyright 1988
Philippine copyright 1988
This edition 1988*

ISBN 0 263 73316 1

*Set in English Times 11 on 12 pt.
03 – 8901 – 51487*

Typeset in Great Britain by JCL Graphics, Bristol

Made and Printed in Great Britain

CHAPTER ONE

THE THEATRE door swung shut with a heavy clunk behind the departing patient. With a weary sigh, Bethany pulled the mask down from her face and stretched.

It was six a.m. and not worth going back to bed.

'One thing about accident call, it certainly gives you short nights.' The speaker, bright red hair standing on end where he had pushed back the green theatre cap, gave Bethany a resigned grin. 'Come on, kid, let's go and find a cup of coffee, and hope the day shift comes on before the next patch-up job comes in.'

'Fine by me.' The nursing team were already moving with brisk efficiency to clear everything up. Bethany offered a grateful smile to her anaesthetic nurse and followed Mark towards the doctors' changing rooms. She would have to call back later and see the patient in the Recovery Room, as the duty anaesthetist always did, but for the moment she could relax.

Fifteen minutes later they were out of theatre greens and boots and on their way down to the canteen through a hospital already stirring to early morning busyness. Mark was making amiable conversation.

'Does it still feel odd to have changed roles in

theatre? Or are you used to it? I can't help feeling even now that it's a crying shame you gave up operating and changed over to anaesthetics!'

'Thanks for the thought, but you know the situation. There just wasn't a job to be had.' There was still an edge of frustration in the memory. A woman surgeon had to be at least twice as good as the men before she could even be considered for a post, and even then a man was usually appointed. Bethany shrugged. 'It took a lot of hard work and extra study to make the switch, so I'm not about to start regretting it,' she said lightly. 'Anyway, I've been a qualified and working anaesthetist for eighteen months now, so why go back over history?'

'How are the promotion prospects? I mean, if you should decide to move from here?'

'Goodness, what did I do this morning to make you want to get rid of me?' She said the words teasingly as they paused at the canteen counter, knowing that she had made no mistakes. Mark was an old friend as well as a working colleague. Bethany shook her head at the offer of breakfast and chose a coffee instead, and they went to sit at a nearby table in the almost-empty echoing spaces, occupied at this time in the day by nothing but a handful of night-shift casualty workers.

'I don't know how you can eat that.' Bethany inspected the greasy sausage and bacon in front of Mark with an amused smile, and stretched like a cat. 'Given that we're not called again, I shall go back to the flat and have my usual cornflakes! I might even manage to have breakfast with Daniel for once, if he's back. He wasn't when I left. In fact, for two people who are living together, we've managed to miss each other remarkably often this last week—they must have had a lot of all-night flaps on in the Path Lab!'

She glanced up from her idle chatter as Mark suddenly pushed his plate away. There was an expression in his eyes quite at variance with his usual lighthearted good humour. His voice held a jerky sympathy. 'Look, Bethany, I do *know*. You don't have to pretend with me. I'm sorry about it. Well, I am and I'm not. But you do seem to be taking it frightfully well——'

'Taking what?' There was a cold frisson down the back of Bethany's neck. One slender hand lifted to push the dark brown hair away from her forehead, as if the heavy wave which flopped down as soon as she removed her theatre cap might cloud her thinking. 'I'm taking what well?' she repeated as he made no answer. 'You haven't heard something I haven't, I suppose? Like, that I'm being made redundant in the latest round of cuts?'

'No, of course not, don't be silly. You're the best emergency anaesthetist we've got. Look, it's all right if you don't want to talk about it, but you don't have to stand on your pride with me. Trisha and I are both thoroughly angry for you, as a matter of fact.' Mark studied the puzzled expression which had crept into the dark brown eyes regarding him, and an almost panicky look suddenly came into his own. 'Oh no! You mean you *don't* know? That's just not possible, everyone else does! Oh, blast Daniel!'

'I think you'd better tell me.' Bethany said through suddenly stiff lips. 'What about Daniel?'

'He's supposed to have moved out on you and in with his latest flame. That's what everyone's saying. They've certainly been seen together a lot, and in—in highly affectionate circumstances.' Mark's helplessness was rapidly changing to anger as he took in the expression on the heart-shaped face in front of him. 'You really didn't know about him and the blonde staff nurse on Med Three, did you? If he *hasn't* moved out he damn well should have! It's not as if it's the first time, but it's certainly the most public. Oh God, now I suppose I've put my foot in my mouth *again!* But I'll say now, I've never the liked the man, and neither has Trisha!'

'It sounds as if I've been living in an ivory tower, what with long theatre hours and everything.' In her stunned state, it was the only thing Bethany could think of to say. She was so dazed she even tried to smile. 'Funny to be the last person to know, isn't it? I suppose you're not making something out of nothing? I mean, as a pathologist he's always around the medical wards a lot. No, all right.' She was wondering with a suddenly nightmarish feeling if she was going to get back to the flat which she had sleepily left in the early hours and find Daniel's clothes missing from the cupboards. She probably wouldn't have noticed. . .'We've been so busy lately we haven't had time to talk,' she offered—but her mind was abruptly caught on, 'It's not as if it's the first time.' And she hadn't known about that, either.

'*Don't* look like that. I wouldn't have raised it at

all if——On the other hand, I'm glad I did!'

'Because as an adult, it's time I stopped being so naïve?' Bethany caught herself up quickly on the words. There was no point in taking it out on Mark. 'I can see now why you thought I might be thinking of looking for a job somewhere else,' she said quickly.

'You certainly don't have to. You're the best accident anaesthetist we've got, as I said, and it helps that you know the other side of the job too, so you always know what's going on!'

'Thanks for the praise. You're pretty good yourself.'

'But I'll still probably be stuck as an ill-paid surgical resistrar for ever, things being what they are. If I weren't a married man I'd be tempted to answer that private-sector ad they've been running lately. Some big engineering company is setting up a special unit for its employees, but it means a lot of travelling, apparently, and it's only on offer to the single. No, don't say it—I know your principles against working in the private sector!'

They were Daniel's principles more than hers, an angry socialism at odds with his fair good looks and smooth manner. Bethany didn't want to bring his name back into it, she just wanted to get away and try to take in the shattering of her private life. She gulped the rest of her tepid coffee and began to stand up. 'I think I'll be off. I'll probably see you later in the day——'

'Probably. Look, are you all right, kid?'

'I'm fine. Don't worry about me. And *kid* is a misnomer. I'm all of twenty-nine.' She walked away

—and tried not to think, abruptly, that Daniel's blonde staff nurse on Med Three was probably several years younger. . .

The same thought came to her mind again when she reached the flat they had shared for the past two years, in a grimy street conveniently close to the hospital. She paused to study herself in the mirror. Small-boned and slight, with a cloud of dark hair framing her face and big brown eyes, she did look younger than her years—until one looked closely and saw the tracery of lines beginning in the delicate skin round the eyes, an extra firmness in the wide mouth. At the moment she had a translucent, washed-out pallor which belied her natural stamina, and the trousers and ill-matched jumper she had pulled on in the early hours scarcely added glamour. Gazed at with critical clarity, who would choose to spend time with someone who looked like a worn, anxious, and definitely ageing ghost?

She turned away sharply with pain squeezing at her heart. Perhaps to Daniel it had never been anything more than temporary. . .Perhaps the whole relationship had merely been born from her passionate desire to please him, that physical fascination he exerted over her which could make her shiver reminiscently even now. And from what Mark had said, Daniel had never been particularly faithful to her at all. So much for her unspoken assumption that they planned to marry eventually, have children, fit a happy family life into a joint successful career . . .

And so much for his backing on her switch from surgery to anaesthetics so that they needn't be parted! It had been at least half her reason for making the change, that she could stay in the same Glasgow hospital as an anaesthetist.

It was better to let anger come than give way to a desperate hurt. By the time Bethany had checked the cupboards to find that some, at least, of Daniel's clothes *were* missing, she could feel the bitter sparkle of it. Maybe he was planning to remove everything bit by bit whenever she was out rather than facing her at all! There *were* other ways, surely, of ending a relationship than simply making a public fool of someone . . .

Abruptly she was across the small sitting room and reaching to search amongst the medical magazines and newspapers which were piled on a coffee table in one corner. What was it Mark had said about an accident job being advertised?

She found it eventually in the local paper after a vain search through everything else. It was listed under 'Classified Jobs—Immediately Available' and was surrounded by a black line to make it stand out.

'Forbes Travis International requires qualified and experienced MRCS for recently established Scottish-based private accident unit. Applicants must be single, 27-33, adaptable, in good health, willing to travel, and free for early appointment to one-year contract. Preliminary enquiries on Glasgow 748320 Ex. 300.'

Bethany's lower lip caught between her teeth. Two years ago—before she had let falling in love conflict with her career—it was the sort of job she might have chased after, whether she had a hope of getting it or not.

Two minutes later she was through to a hotel. A
moment after that, her crisp enquiry for extension
300 brought a ringing sound, then a click and a deep
voice saying simply, 'Yes?'

'I'm ringing in answer to your advertisement for
an MRCS to do accident work. My name's Dale. I
have the relevant qualifications. Perhaps you could
tell me whether the job's already filled?'

'You don't wast any time, Miss Dale. Still, that's
all to the good. Have you had much accident
experience?'

The deep voice was as crisp as hers had been, and
its owner hadn't automatically backed off from her
enquiry because her own voice was female. 'Yes,
several years,' Bethany began. She glanced absently
at her watch, then realised the reason for his first
comment. It was still only seven a.m. 'I apologise for
ringing so early,' she went on quickly, 'but I've just
finished a casualty shift in theatre. If I woke you I'm
sorry——'

'No problem. What was your case?'

'Excision of a ruptured spleen after an
RTA—road traffic accident. I was——'

'It's all right, you needn't translate. Was it
satisfactory?'

'Yes, thank you.'

'Good. The type of work our unit's set up to
handle is site accidents, but if you've been used to
RTAs it's much the same, general accident surgery.
One thing I have to point out, though, is that you
could find yourself working in temporary theatres.

Would that faze you?'

'I shouldn't think so. In fact it sounds interesting.'

'Do you ever suffer from motion or travel sickness?'

'I never have, so far——'

'Then it sounds worthwhile our meeting. Could you come in at eleven this morning to the Grand Hotel, McQuarry Street?'

'Yes, I—should be able to manage that.' She could if she went back to the hospital now to do her morning round, arranged for someone to stand in for her, got a rapid leave of temporary absence, in fact got everything swiftly organised. With determination it should be possible.

'Good, I'll see you then. Ask at the desk for Forbes Travis International or for Mr Jardine's room and they'll tell you where to go. Until later, Miss Dale.'

There was click and he was gone, leaving Bethany with her thoughts whirling. There had been no time to tell him that she had been working as an anaesthetist rather than a surgeon for the past year and a half—but did it matter? He hadn't given out much information himself; who exactly, for instance, would she be seeing?

For an exploratory meeting perhaps that didn't matter either, Bethany told herself, and resisted the temptation to visualise the face and form behind that deep, curt, slightly abrasive voice. The important thing was that he hadn't rejected her enquiries out of hand!

Caution with a cynical edge had taken the place of optimism by the time she was walking up McQuarry

Street at ten forty-five, respectably clad in grey skirt and jacket with an eye to looking efficient, and with her CV tucked in her handbag. It cost them nothing to see her and the Sex Discrimination Act prevented them from rejecting her sight unseen. Being given more than token consideration for a job was another matter. Still, she was here and could at least listen while someone told her yet again that her record was good, and then gave the job to a man.

It was funny, even if not amusing, that when the powers-that-be decreed that 'women didn't have the stamina to be surgeons' they never considered the long hours theatre *nurses* spent on their feet!

CHAPTER TWO

SHE WALKED in through the hotel entrance, flanked with tall marble pillars to make it as grand as its name but with a great deal of modern plate-glass on show to bring it up to date. It was one of Glasgow's smarter hotels and smelled of money. An acre of shining marble led her to a curving reception desk clad in dark panelling, and a reception clerk looked up at her enquiry.

'Forbes Travis International? Ah yes, Doctor. . .?'

'Dale. I was told to ask for Mr Jardine's room?'

'Mr Jardine's suite,' the clerk corrected her with a touch of reproof, and flicked his fingers towards a nearby uniformed page. 'First floor, Doctor, Jamie will show you the way. Excuse me, now——' and he picked up a telephone as it rang.

Bethany followed Jamie across another acre of marble to the lift and wondered if she was supposed to tip him for escorting her. Probably not, and she hadn't any change on her anyway. A glance around suggested Forbes Travis International were picking up a heavy tab, and the fact that the clerk had unerringly identified her as 'Doctor' without being told suggested that there had been a procession of hopeful surgeons in and out of here. That certainly made her chances the less. Nevertheless she squared her slim shoulders and followed the page along the thickly-carpeted first-floor corridor until he opened a door for her without knocking and ushered her inside.

The first shock was to find herself in the company of three others, not sitting round having a discussion but placed at a careful distance from each other on the seats around the room with the very obvious air of waiting to be called. They were various sizes and shapes but all young and all male, and wearing expressions from carefully casual to determinedly confident. The second shock was when one of them looked across at her and spoke.

'Ah, another victim for the interviews? This is the last day, so if it was five yesterday and five today, that makes the odds at ten to one!'

He was very large, very blond, and had a slightly fractured accent with what sounded like Scandinavian overtones. He also seemed extremely cheerful and exuded good health. 'Only one of us can get the well-paid job, I suppose,' he went on with undimmed good will. 'Two of us have been in, one's in now, and me not. I'm next, I think. Have a seat!'

'If they're actually going to decide today at least that's something,' one of the others put in, glancing up. He added pointedly, 'And I suppose they are, since I was told to wait!'

His eyes had assessed Bethany and, she was almost sure, dismissed her as no competition. That was enough to make her shut her mouth, when she had been opening it to say that she had only come to find out about the job, not to be interviewed for it. On the other hand if this really was the last day of the interviews, the voice on the telephone's 'You don't waste time' took on a new and sarcastic meaning. Well, he had invited her to come, anyway. She sat down abruptly and tried to look unflustered.

But if it *was* an interview and she had come to it completely cold——

Her thoughts were interrupted by an opening door and another young male emerged, looking set-faced as if things hadn't gone well but trying to smile at the very smooth-looking business-suited man who came out with him and was offering him a hand to shake. 'Nice of you to come, and I'm sorry the personal factors don't fit in with our plans,' the latter said with apparent sincerity and in a noticeably American accent. 'Very good to meet you all the same. Ah, now, Dr Lindstrom, would you care to come along in——?'

The blond Scandinavian got cheerfully to his feet and proved to be even larger standing up. Good for orthopaedics, Bethany thought, drily as the tide of his passing practically seemed to blow her back into her chair. She was trying not to let her heart sink. If the voice had called her to interview without even knowing much about her (except that she'd just come off a casualty shift) then it did look very much as if she was only here as a token.

The set-faced one had left. Time passed, only broken by the other one who had spoken to her addressing her suddenly with, 'He's FTI's personnel man—the Yank you just saw—in case it helps to know,' and then lapsing into silence again. The other man present simply sat, studying his fingernails as if they were of riveting interest.

Nothing could be heard from the next room, so the hotel's sound proofing must be good. Finally—and after what seemed an age, so that Bethany began to worry about her stand-in at the hospital—the door opened again, the young giant Dr Lindstrom emerged looking as cheerful as when he went in, and Bethany found herself being addressed with smooth politeness.

'Dr Dale? I believe Dr Jardine put you in at the last minute. Do come in, won't you?'

It was a smaller sitting-room, unrelievedly chintzy and with three armchairs arranged in an arc to face the fourth. Two of the armchairs were occupied. In one, a grey-haired man of patrician countenance looked a combination of neat, rich and kindly and began to get to his feet with instant courtesy; but it was the man who rose more slowly from the other chair who took Bethany's eyes.

His hair had the blue-black sheen of a raven's wing but was cropped close against his head. Lean features accentuated the shadows under his cheekbones. He was no more than medium height but close-knit and muscular with wide powerful shoulders, and he exuded a force-field of magnetism which would draw anyone to look at him. Most striking of all were his eyes, an impossible bright blue which seemed to gleam in his lean face with the brilliance of sapphires.

Bethany gulped instinctively.

'Miss Dale? Thank you for coming.' It was the same voice she had heard on the telephone, deep and slightly abrasive. 'We assumed you were interested in the job by your calling, but I'm aware you don't know any of the details yet. However, since today was, we hope, our last day——'

'Oh, I think we could say definitely our last day, Neil,' the patrician gentleman put in. He had a gentle voice with a soft American accent less pronounced than the one who had show Bethany in, and he smiled as he turned to her. 'Thank you for coming at such short notice, Dr Dale—or do you prefer Miss, in the English fashion? I gather your surgeons do that here. Please do sit down—and as we haven't any papers on you, have you perhaps got a list of your qualifications and experience?'

Bethany handed them over and tried to pull herself together. Goodness knows she had been to enough interviews. . .The patrician gentleman was addressing her again, with a kindly and almost confiding smile which made her feel he wanted nothing more than to put her at her ease.

'My name is Travis, Dr Dale, and the gentleman at the end is David Kerr, but you can ignore us in the main because we merely represent the company. Dr Jardine is our chief surgeon in charge of the project and he'll be asking you all the relevant questions.' He twinkled at her, probably well aware that she could see out of the corner of her eye the way the other two were quickly running through the sheets she had handed over. 'However, while they're looking at what I'm sure are your excellent qualifications, perhaps I could give you a general outline of our ideas for our accident unit.'

'Yes, please.'

'FTI is an engineering conglomerate and we do a great deal of site work. We also believe in offering our employees the best possible conditions of work.' He made the statement as if it could be taken for granted. 'Naturally every person who works for us has private medical insurance taken out by the company, and in addition there is at least some medical facility on every site—but, of necessity, our site crews often work in remote places. Now, whole we do have a good accident record—' he stressed that firmly and then allowed a look of regret to wash over his features—'there can be surgical emergencies.'

'I'd imagine so,' Bethany put in obediently as he paused.

'Quite. I'm sure you must know the dangers of moving some types of injury. It has therefore occurred to us to set up a pilot project where accident surgeons can be taken to the site of an accident rather than the other way round. We have the transport and radio facilities; we also have a recently renovated property here in Scotland to act as our central point——'

'Why Scotland?'

'A relevant question,' he said, rather in the tone of one patting a good child on the head. 'With the type of transportation we envisage, the Scottish

Highlands make a good hub for this particular operation. FTI currently has several gas and oil explorations going on in your North Sea. Then to the west we have working sites in Greenland, Canada and Alaska.' While Bethany was still trying to take in the distances involved he added, 'Now, has anything you've heard so far put you off, Dr Dale?'

'No, not at all. You're setting up a—a team of flying surgeons, is that it?'

'Precisely. A small group with good accident experience, ready to travel anywhere at any time. That's why our advertisements have stressed youth as well as experience—for adaptability and good health. David, have you anything to put in at this point?'

'No, chief, I think you've covered the basics.' The man who had been identified for her as the personnel officer answered respectfully. The glance he gave Bethany was noncommital enough to damp, just a little, the surge of adrenalin which was sweeping through her. This wasn't just a job, it was a thoroughly exciting one . . . one she'd give her eye-teeth to be involved in, and one she was sure she could do.

'I'm sure Dr Dale will forgive me if I mention that she doesn't look like my immediate idea of a surgeon,' the older man put in at that moment, though when her eyes jerked to his face he was twinkling at her again to take the sting out of his words. Bethany couldn't resist giving him a prompt answer.

'Surgery doesn't have to be a question of brute force, Mr Travis. I'm a great deal tougher than I look, as my experience will show! I can provide good references.' One of them was her professor of surgery and she hoped that the man in the middle at least had noted his eminent name. She finished pointedly, 'Contrary to popular opinion, too, women come out very well in stamina tests!'

'I believe they do. I'm always saying that we should try to recruit more women as engineers.' The old man answered her amicably and then turned his head towards the black-haired man. 'Now I'll turn you over to Dr Jardine—Neil?'

Bethany had been involuntarily aware of him all through the last few minutes, and of the way those electric-blue eyes had been scanning the pages of her CV. She had known, when the delicately-etched black brows had snapped together in a brief frown, what he was probably looking at, and was ready for his first question. She wasn't quite ready for the way the incredible blue of his eyes seemed to pin her to her chair, and her fingers made an involuntary smoothing movement against the grey suit material of her skirt.

'I see you've taken a qualification in anaesthetics as well as your MRCS. Which have you been doing lately, anaesthetics or surgery?'

'Anaesthetics. It was a question of job opportunities.' To her relief he accepted that with a brief nod, and she added quickly, 'But surgery's my main interest and I'd like to get back into it.'

'Right. Tell me what you'd do with a patient presenting an obvious fractured scapula, shallow breathing, thready pulse, and coma.'

'First check for other injuries, specifically any pressure fracture to the skull.' It felt like a challenge delivered in that abrasive deep voice and with those sapphire eyes boring into her, and Bethany responded to it as such instinctively. It was more like taking an examination than having a job interview as he flung other suggested cases at her. Once or twice she felt a stir of resentment as she was aware he was trying to catch her out; once or twice she stuck to her guns when he queried a theoretical diagnosis and met his frown coolly. She had begun to feel she had a score to settle with him anyway for letting her come to this cold without warning—and he would be no slouch to work for, that was for sure—but she was also beginning to hope burningly that she *wasn't* just here as a 'token woman', and she was out to prove that she could do this job as well as anyone. *Better*.

Abruptly he sat back from his gruelling series of questions and regarded her with, she could swear, a touch of mockery.

'All right. You don't let having been up half the night cloud your thinking, that's for sure!'

She had almost forgotten she had been. The remark gave her quiver of hope. 'You can see I haven't lost touch through working in anaesthetics either,' she countered promptly.

'Hm. Would you be prepared to work for us as an anaesthetist, if that was what was on offer?'

'Yes, I—I suppose so. Though I'd rather get back to surgery. I didn't realise——'

'I think we're set up in the anaesthetics field, Neil.'

That was the personnel officer putting in his pennyworth. Bethany had almost forgotten his presence. 'In fact with today's appointment we'll have all the team.'

'No harm in checking. One last question for Miss Dale and I've finished. I presume you haven't any marriage plans?'

'No, I haven't,' Bethany told him crisply. Her chin came up. 'In addition, I wouldn't be prepared to let any personal relationship interfere with my career!'

'That *is* a question we've had to ask our male applicants too,' the elderly man, Mr Travis, put in quickly in his gentle voice, as if to reassure her that no discrimination was involved. 'In fact the last candidate but one had a fiancée and we felt it ruled him out. One thing I did wonder, Dr Dale, is how you'd feel as the odd one out, so to speak? I don't know if I made it clear, but as the team is on permanent call, you'd be living as well as working with the rest of the group.'

'I don't think I'd cause any disruptions.'

There was a sudden unexpected laugh from Neil Jardine. Perhaps it had been drawn forth by her blunt answer and her dry tone. His lean features seemed to change with humour and his eyes were still glinting as he sobered. 'I think the chief wondered if you'd feel uncomfortable,' he suggested. 'And—since you've shown so much interest in the job—your answer would undoubtedly be no, whether true or not. Right, I haven't got anything else, so . . . ?'

The others shook their heads. All of them got to their feet. Bethany was asked politely if she would mind waiting in the next room. Then she was outside again, back with the other interviewees whose heads jerked up at her arrival; and she sat down with her hands gripped together.

Mr Travis was on her side, she thought. She had the sense that the personnel man had been against her and preferred some other candidate. With Neil Jardine it was impossible to know. He would presumably have the casting vote when he was the one with the professional knowledge.

And they were actually going to decide here and now. She would do better not to sit here holding her breath. It was ridiculous anyway, she hadn't even heard of the job until this morning; didn't know either what the strength of the opposition was against her.

It had quite gone from her mind that she had only come here as a chance to get away from the hospital and from Daniel. She was caught up in a yearning for the job itself and its challenge and interest. . .

The door opened, bringing all eyes round on to it. Bethany knew at once, because the personnel man's glance didn't meet her own. He turned to the giant young Scandinavian and said smoothly, 'Dr Lindstrom, our congratulations, and would you come back in? Thank you for coming, everybody else, and we'll be sending you an official letter, of course.'

There would be other jobs to chase after and not get—but Bethany felt the sharp sting of disappointment.

CHAPTER THREE

AT LEAST the impetus of taking herself off for an interview had set Bethany into action. She found it quite easy to pack up Daniel's possessions, plant them in the hallway outside the flat, and have the locks changed. She left a note on top of them saying. 'I think you get the point,' and buried herself in work.

They met, of course. It was unavoidable. It was also unavoidable that Bethany's heart turned over involuntarily when grey eyes looked down into her own with an expression between anger and sheepishness and he protested. 'That was a bit drastic, wasn't it?'

'When something's over it's over——'

'And when someone comes to you with tales about me you believe 'em? Yes, I thought it was that! Well, Beth, let me tell you——'

'No, don't tell me *anything*. You never have before! But just because I don't usually have my ear to the ground it doesn't mean I'm completely *dim*.' She had to whip herself into anger to counter the pain of it, the desire to touch him when he thrust a long-fingered hand through his fair hair in an oh-so-familiar gesture. She had always loved his tallness which dwarfed her, the willowy shape of him, the little bump at the bridge of his nose which made his profile not quite perfect. In their early days she used to tease him for being far too-good looking for his own good. 'There's nothing else to say,' she told him curtly, and began to turn away, to escape.

'Really? *I've* got plenty else to say! You never think anything could be your fault, do you? When did you last bother to do yourself up to come to a party with me? When did you last bother to put on make-up *at all*, for that matter? Or get your hair decently done, or buy a frilly nightie——'

'*What?*' His words brought her round on him in a rage. 'I'm a working doctor, not a doll! We're both doctors! Do *I* complain about the times when you don't shave?'

'No, because you like it. Anyway, that's a different point——'

'I'm not getting into a domestic wrangle with you.' Bethany was desperately short of breath. 'Just get out of my way, right? As for my hair, I'll get it cut short like a punk and dyed purple if I feel like it—or not if I don't—but it certainly won't be for your benefit, it'll be for my own!'

'Not if you have it dyed purple at your age, darling,' Daniel said nastily, and then caught himself up with a hand reaching for her. 'No, look, I didn't mean that—Beth come on, I know I've been . . .'

'We haven't anything further to say to each other.'

'Then don't blame me if I go where I'm appreciated!'

'I don't. I just felt you should take your luggage with you—all of it!'

With that she escaped, shaking inside and surprised it hadn't shown in the tartness of her voice. It had been on the tip of her tongue to say that she hoped

they'd all be very happy—him, his staff nurse, and all
her rows of false eyelashes. Just as well she hadn't; she
could at least try to keep the rags of her dignity.

After that she avoided him studiously and observed
painfully that he was going out of his way to be seen,
but also to be seen ignoring her. It made venturing
into the doctors' common room a chore. It gave her
an even greater longing to be out of this hospital
too—in spite of the warming discovery of how many
friends she had, who would come up particularly to
talk to her, and wall her around in the centre of a
group if Daniel was anywhere about.

It was only a week since it had all happened, but the
days and nights seemed to crawl as if the clocks were
being run by snails. Then, suddenly, everything
changed.

When the letter arrived on her dormat with FTI in a
triangular logo on the white envelope, Bethany
assumed it was her official turn-down. The sight of it
brought back the churning disappointment which she
had tried to crush all week. She put the envelope
down, then made herself pick it up again and slit it
open. The top sheet of white paper wasn't in the
expected typescript but, surprisingly, in a forceful
black handwriting.

'Dear Miss Dale,

'Forbes Travis International is prepared to
offer you a year's contract as an anaesthetist if
you would like to consider taking this post. It has
been agreed that you would be the best candidate
owing to your surgical experience.

'We need someone as soon as possible, so if

you are still free and would be willing to take the job, please get in touch immediately.

'Yours sincerely, Neil Jardine.'

The letter fluttered to the floor from her nerveless fingers. Then she was swooping down to seize it up again and re-read it, her heart thumping madly.

Anaesthetist rather than a surgeon . . .

But it was the offer of a job; a job with the mobile accident service which had so caught at her imagination!

She flicked rapidly over the second sheet attached to the first. This one *was* typed, and it was a contract. It had her name filled in. It also stated a rate of pay which was enough to make her jaw drop. Goodness, if *that* was what was offered in the private sector . . .

The money wasn't important, a bonus rather than an incentive, even if thinking so made her less practical than she should be. The main point was the job. Bethany turned back to the first page again. The handwriting made it read like a personal invitation.

That was a ridiculous thought; but the bold sharpness of the writing brought a clear picture of raven-black hair, the lean planes of a face, a thin mobile mouth and a tough jaw. And vivid, electric-blue eyes.

He'd probably be a bastard to work for, Bethany's mind told her warningly, even while the blood surged along her veins in a race of triumph. *And* he'd turned her down as a surgeon after all his deliberately tough questions. Looked at closely, the phraseology of 'it has been agreed' could even suggest that it wasn't his choice at all. Maybe she had 'the chief', Mr Travis to thank for this offer. After all, he had said something about wishing he could recruit more women engineers, so maybe it was he who wanted a demonstrably mixed team.

Still and all, there was absolutely no way she was going to turn it down!

The next couple of hours had her checking her availability—and talking the hospital into letting her go in less than three weeks because that made the end of the month. Then she made the vital telephone call.

It was to somewhere called Achnabrae House, since that was the address on top of Neil Jardine's letter; although FTI's company addresses were in New York and The Hague. Achnabrae appeared to be in the Scottish Highlands. As the phone was picked up she heard the familiar deep abrasive voice. Neil Jardine seemed to count answering the telephone amongst his duties.

'It's yes? Good. Oh, no sooner than that? Well, we must take the best we can. Send your contract to the Dutch office, signed, and they'll ratify it and send you back a copy. They'll also give you proper directions for getting here.'

'Here?'

'To Achnabrae. You'll need a car; there's a tiny village a couple of miles down the hill, apart from that the house is miles from anywhere. By ground transport, that is. As the chopper flies is something else again, naturally.'

It didn't seem particularly natural to Bethany, but she felt an inevitable stir of excitement at the thought that that was how they would go out on call. At least as far as the nearest airport . . . She came back to herself as he asked crisply, 'Any questions so far?'

'Where do we live?'

'In the house. The radio room's here and so are we. Living quarters: small flatlets, but a communal dining-room for eating in, and there are various other facilities. Anything else you want to ask?'

A million things, but his curt manner was catching. 'Clothing?' Bethany enquired crisply.

'Workwise, tracksuits for flying and a thick jacket. *Very* thick, look for something padded. We'll have disposable theatre gear to take round with us. Otherwise whatever you normally wear off duty, as long as that isn't very high heels. Unless you like sinking your stilettos into moorland,' There was a mocking edge on the deep voice, but he was going on before Bethany could retort. 'You're joining us as an anaesthetist, so I don't suppose you've got any personal equipment. Everything you'll need is here. The Dutch office will let you know if you need any extra vaccinations or shots. I think that's all.' He added, 'Your references checked out well, by the way, except that Professor Main didn't know you'd switched to anaesthetics. He thought it was a pity but could understand your reasoning.' And then he was gone, brisk as ever and leaving her with the finality of a click in her ear as he rang off.

It was done—she'd accepted and was in! She decided abruptly that she must look Neil Jardine up in the medical directory. It was idiotic to work with a man not knowing his qualifications.

When she found them, they were impressive enough to make her purse her lips in a low whistle. So what was *he* doing running a small private accident unit, when with that bunch of letters after his name, he surely might have been a high-powered consultant somewhere running his own hospital department? She could think of several teaching hospitals which would fall over backwards to get him. Neuro-surgery seemed to be—or have been—his particular speciality. At least up to four years ago: there was nothing listed since then.

Thinking about him, she decided he might easily be the type not to bother to fill in extra forms to bring his entry up to date. She also saw that from the dates given he must be thirty-five-two years older than the specifics advertised. As he was the team's head, perhaps they didn't apply to him. Presumably it did apply to him, though, not to be married or engaged?

She closed the heavy volume sharply. Her curiosity was feeling suspiciously like personal interest. As the memory of Neil Jardine's extreme magnetism caught her it almost gave her pause. Then, with a familiar and bitter twist to her heart, she could assure herself that after Daniel, she was inured to men as men.

In stark contrast to the past week's crawl, the next few weeks seemed to rush. Bethany kept quiet about her plans except to a very close few. She knew word would get round eventually, but she didn't want to hear the gossips murmur pityingly that she was running away. It was bad enough to have far too many sightings of Daniel in the company of Med Three's blonde staff nurse with her prettily doll-like appearance and her obvious devotion.

Suddenly it was her last day. Her packing and shopping were done. She had had to quell the doubts which kept creeping in to war with her excitement. At first she had wanted to slide out of goodbyes and simply disappear, but at the last moment Mark insisted on having an impromptu farewell party for her in the doctors' common room.

It wasn't an invitation party and people were simply milling in and out with several of them on call anyway. A warming number of her colleagues seemed to have made a point of being present, however. Things were well under way when she felt Mark stiffen, and glancing round, she saw who had just come in, tall and fair and willowy and with that unmistakable profile.

Daniel was, presumably, on his way somewhere else. He was obviously not on duty since he was sporting his party-going gear of trendy faded jeans and a black leather jacket. He had his blonde with him too, which brought forth a mutter from Mark.

'Surely he wouldn't dare! He can stay *that* end of the room and not at *our* party——'

'This place is public property to doctors. Don't worry about it. I'm not.' Bethany managed to make her voice flippant. She had officially finished work, so she was dressed up for once—deliberately, keeping the flag flying—in a way she hadn't for months: a swirling skirt with an informal strappy top which was a vivid raspberry shade, and long dangly earrings to set off her new short hairstyle. She had already had compliments on that, and on the way it accentuated her heart-shaped face with its good cheekbones. Carefully applied make-up lent the big brown eyes a sparkle, and they were alight anyway with the awed good wishes her friends had been giving her now that the adventurous details of her new job were finally out.

'Don't play mother hen, Mark,' she murmured to him as he stirred resentfully with a glare in Daniel's direction. 'After all—' her voice lifted on a lilt—'I'm off tomorrow to this remote Highland manor—well, relatively remote, with all that helicopter transport we'll apparently have when we're on call!'

'Not to mention private jets standing by to carry you off to Canada, etc.,' someone put in. 'Where *did* you find this extraordinary job, Bethany?'

'In the local paper, believe it or not. Not that they weren't recruiting all over the place, I gather. Certainly one of the team's Scandinavian, he was at interview the same time as me——'

She saw out of the corner of her eye that someone was talking to Daniel. And that he was looking blank and disbelieving suddenly. She turned her shoulder quickly and went on talking. 'Anyway from the Further Details sheet FTI's Dutch office sent me, we're quite an international bunch,' she went on in tones of deliberate amusement. 'One of the surgeons is listed as a New Zealander, as well as the giant Swede I was just telling you about!'

'Bethany? I want a word with you!'

She had to turn round. Anyway, long fingers seized her arm to spin her towards him. 'Oh really, Daniel, do you?' she managed with an admirable coolness. '*If* you could avoid grabbing me by the elbow like that . . . No, it's all right everyone, so just keep talking and drinking!'

She managed to speak first as they reached the

corner; managed too to shake off the fingers which were biting into her arm, by detaching herself with a very obvious politeness. 'Now you're here we can talk about the flat,' she told him limpidly. 'The lease is in our joint names, remember? I was going to leave you a note with the keys to suggest that you might like to take it over. I'll be out of it in the morning——'

'So you really *are* leaving! I'd only just heard! Look, this is ridiculous——'

'What is, why? I've got the offer of a good job and I'm going to take it. You're surely not going to suggest I should have *consulted* you?'

The grey eyes flickered but were still angry. And disbelieving. And then, caressing. 'Beth, honey, don't do this. We can still work it out. You're looking really gorgeous—like the Sleeping Beauty awoken, as a matter of fact——'

'You know, I've never really liked having my name shortened. Like you not wanting to be called Dan.' Her voice was sweetly conversational, even if somewhere inside her there was a weakening quiver, and then a memory to grate along her nerves. 'We were talking about the flat,' she said on a breath, 'and if you don't want to take it over I suggest you dispose of it. There are always people looking. That newly-married psychiatric registrar might be interested, I should think.'

'Beth. *Bethany,*' Daniel corrected himself appealingly at her carefully raised eyebrow. 'I know you're only doing this because of me. Why do you have to be so impulsive? People split up all the time and then realise——'

'I'm taking the job because it's a damn good one and exciting and the chance of a lifetime! Haven't you heard the details? Oh, I'm surprised, everyone's talking about it.' She was glad to be able to deliver that little lie and imply that everyone else had known for ages, when she thought what else everyone had talked about. 'It really is the best thing that's happened to me for years!'

'Time you came back to the party, kid,' Mark's voice said behind her, and she felt his arm slide round her waist. 'It's bad enough to have our best—and best-looking—anaesthetist leaving us for the glamour of private work, without your hiding in a corner instead of saying your proper goodbyes!'

'*Private* work? You mean you're taking yourself off to the private sector?' Daniel's expression had taken on a look of thunder, and his voice was scathing. 'After all we've said—against all possible *principles*? My God, Beth, whatever the situation, you can't sell out! And I'll say here and now, if that's what you're doing I really have finished with you!'

'Funny, I thought it was she who'd finished with you.' Mark said in a tone of mild interest. 'And haven't you mislaid someone in your uninvited travels down to this end of the room? At least, I thought I lip-read someone saying "Danny" protestingly as you dropped her like a hot coal a few minutes ago! Come on, Bethany, there's lots of people waiting to drink your health and wish you wild success!'

'You said what the job was deliberately to annoy him,' Bethany hissed between her teeth as he moved her firmly away. If she hadn't been so shaken by conflicting emotions inside she'd have wanted to giggle. Perhaps with an edge of hysteria. 'And does she really call him Danny? Oh dear, oh dear, he hates that!'

'Why should you care? So for God's sake stop caring. I came to rescue you because I know your face too well, kid . . .' And then Mark had swept her back amongst the crowd, pushed a glass of champagne in her hand from a bottle specially bought in her honour, and the celebrations were continuing. When she did get time to look round, Daniel had gone.

And well rid. She knew that perfectly well. She had a drive to do tomorrow up into the Scottish Highlands and then a new place to live, a new and challenging job, new people to work with. It was all terrific. She didn't intend to let it stop being terrific.

She kept the mood firmly in place as she set off the next morning for the drive northwards in the car she had bought, second-hand but in good condition and a little sportier than anything she'd usually have chosen. Or have been able to afford. She wasn't going to start feeling guilty about that, either, just because she had heard so many of Daniel's arguments about accepting poverty because of the importance of free medicine for all . . . She wrenched her mind away quickly and thought instead, determinedly, that with her year's contract with FTI safely ratified, she wouldn't have to worry about finding the HP payments.

She looked resolutely forward instead of back. It would be pleasant to see the giant young Dr

Lindstrom again (Erik, from the information list) and she wondered what he was like as a surgeon. He must be good since he had won the job. Her lips curved in a sudden appreciative grin: however would they fit him into a helicopter? Well, no doubt she'd find out, when she had to travel with him!

Who else was there that she'd have to get to know? Lang Graham, the New Zealand surgeon. Another anaesthetist, listed as Peter Llewellyn, probably Welsh with a name like that. That appeared to be the team, three surgeons and two anaesthetists. No specialist theatre nurses, she'd noted, either male *or* female; so she had to suppose there were suitably trained nursing staff available in the first-aid posts on the sites.

Then there were the radio operators; and presumably there must be pilots to fly everyone in and out.

Excitement stirred in her again. All in all, it was quite a party.

And, of course, there was the dynamic, highly qualified, and slightly mysterious Neil Jardine.

CHAPTER FOUR

IF THERE hadn't been a discreet notice in FTI's triangular logo, Bethany wouldn't have known she was arriving at the right place. A long drive wound away uphill and disappeared behind a line of pine-trees fanned out like a row of sentinels against the delicate blue of the sky, but if there was a house up there it was invisible from here.

The last few miles had been distinctly scenic, with a clarity in the air which invigorated Bethany's nerves into a fizzing energy. The gleam of a loch here, a distant misty blue of hills there, a rolling emptiness of rock and moorland had broken out around her a bare mile beyond the last small township on her route map. There could scarcely have been a greater contrast to the grimy, familiar sprawl of Glasgow's city and the poorer area of it in which the hospital was situated.

As she approached Achnabrae village—a few cottages snuggled against a hillside, with two pubs and the unexpected plate-glass window of a supermarket—it had been difficult to remind herself in practical terms that setting up a business venture amongst all this spacious beauty had probably qualified FTI for a development grant. Or for that matter that there was an international airport a mere hop away as the helicopter flew.

She negotiated the rising slope of the drive with a suitable care for its uneven surface, and as she reached the crest through a gap in the pines the house was there in front of her.

Its elegance was a surprise. It looked like someone's country seat, with a graciously square Georgian front and a jumble of roofs behind to show where additions had been made to the rear of the building. Tall gracefully proportioned windows balanced a central front door and caught the glint of the afternoon sun, shining like watchful eyes. The crest of the hill had been flattened to surround the house with well-kept lawns. Below that, an area of parkland dropped to a valley which rose again towards distant blue hills dreaming on the horizon.

Bethany's mouth formed an O of awed pleasure, and then curved into amusement. *This* was where she was going to live?

She pulled efficiently to a halt on a newly-laid sweep of gravel which led to the carved oak front door. She had to stifle a grin when she caught herself thinking she really ought to be at some servants' entrance. It was definitely easier to imagine a butler behind that front door and a kilted laird somewhere within than the head-quarters of a high-powered accident unit. There should be well-worn antique furniture, bagpipes hung on the wall, and *dogs,* rather than long-distance radio equipment and emergency surgical packs and autoclave facilities and . . .'

She shook her head with a smile to clear the dreams out of it, and moved lightly to rap on a heavy knocker which proved to be all the door offered by way of signalling her arrival.

The door opened while she was still knocking. Erik Lindstrom, looking even larger than she remembered and showing a vast amount of muscular brown leg in running shorts, beamed sunnily down at her from his great height.

'Hello again! I'm passing the window and see you coming. Welcome—I came a week ago and now we're at full numbers!' His Swedish lilt sounded even stronger than she recollected, but his cheerful good nature seemed to be a permanent feature. 'We breathe good air here, ho?' he enquired amiably with an approving gesture at the view, and stood aside for her to enter. 'Come on in, Bet'anee, I'm Erik in case you don't remember, and I'll show you where to find Neil!'

Informality was obviously the order of the day. Bethany gave him a smile and stepped inside. She had the brief impression of the polished wood of a hall and an open door beyond it gave the glimpse of filtered sunshine and light furnishings. There was the murmur of male voices and a clicking sound. Her stomach gave a slight clench of nervousness, but Erik was going on speaking.

'You can park round the back in the garages and come in and out of the side door, you'll see when you're shown round. There have been calls already, the others were working before we got here, but no one's out at the moment, so come and meet Lang and Peter. You two, here's our other anaesthetist——'

'Bethany Dale. Hi.'

They were apparently passing time by playing a game of snooker on a half-size table set just round the corner from the door. Lang was loose-limbed, mousy-haired, and casual-looking. He paused in his contemplation of the snooker table to give her a sharp look and a cool, 'Hi, nice to meet you, I'm Lang Graham.' Peter had fair curly hair which made a contrast against faintly olive skin. He was nearest and moved to offer a hand to shake.

'Hallo. We're in the same line. It's going to be useful that there's two of us. Where've you been working?'

'Glasgow. Emergency work mainly. Did Erik say just now you've been out on call from here already? What's it like?'

'Better than working in a war zone. I've been in Lebanon recently. I'm a quarter Lebanese,' Peter added as if by way of explanation. He glanced across at Erik. 'Are you going to buzz Neil on the internal phone to tell him our last team member's arrived, or take her along to his office?'

'No need, I'm here.'

The deep voice almost made Bethany jump. He had come in from behind her and as she turned she had the impression again, of reined-in dynamism. His clothes were as casual as those of the others. light slacks which clung to his lean hips and a blue T-shirt which looked pale in contrast to the vivid sapphire eyes. The blue-black raven's-wing hair lay close against his head but had ruffled to a slight curl. There was a curl to the corners of his lips too as he regarded Bethany with one eyebrow raised.

'It's your bright scarlet car outside, is it? It looks more serviceable than Lang's heavily-in-hock Lamborghini, but you'd have done better with a four-wheel-drive round here!'

'Lay off. He who criticises my car criticises my life,' Lang drawled good-humouredly, and executed a neat round-the-table shot which clicked the ball into a pocket.

'It's your suspension. Bethany—Beth?'

'Bethany. I'll answer to the other if you yell it at me in an emergency, though.'

'I snap rather than yell. Welcome to Achnabrae, and come and be shown round. The official bits, round the back and down in the cellars, are heavily computerised,. but the rest of it has a more human touch. I'll show you your flat and then we'll go all round and I'll introduce you to the radio boys——'

He was interrupted by a sharp buzz from somewhere. He was in immediate fluid motion and she saw him lift a telephone receiver from an unobtrusive bracket on the wall.

'Yes, I'm here,' he said crisply, and Bethany was aware that all the others had paused to listen.

'On which, Rig Two? Tell then to scramble a chopper for fifteen minutes. No, tell them it's what we're here for, just as much as the heavy jobs! Mark it in for me and . . . Dr Dale, the new anaesthetist. She's here, so I'll take her along.'

'I can do it with you, Neil. Let the poor girl settle in!'

'I'm choosing to throw her in at the deep end,

thanks, Peter. It's good practice.' Neil Jardine's voice
brooked no argument, but the sapphire glance he sent
Bethany was challenging. 'Unless you can't cope after
the drive? But you haven't exactly come from the ends
of the earth, so I'd imagine you can!'

'Certainly. I'll just need——'

'Your flying jacket if you can fish it out quickly.
Otherwise I'll find you a spare. You're dressed all right
otherwise.' He regarded her smart fawn slacks and
green shirt with an impersonal eye which very
obviously took more account of their serviceability
than of whether they suited her or not. 'Come with me
and I'll gen you up while the chopper's arriving. It's a
rig worker with a crushed hand, impact injury, simple
fractures. I'll show you where the anaesthesia stores
are kept. Better choose some alternatives in case he
turns out to be allergic to something.'

'Of course.' She'd have liked to add, *no need to tell
me my job,* but she bit her tongue on it. It would be
no way to start and particularly not with the others
listening. Her heart had given a sharp thud when he
gave her name to the radio operator and her pulse was
now racing, but she was determined to show nothing
but calm. As he moved she followed him with a
deliberate air of cool efficiency.

'Lang, you're in charge if another emergency comes
in while I'm out. OK. . .'

The next hours were a confused mass of
impressions for Bethany. To add to that she was making a rigid attempt to look as unflappable as if all this
happened to her every day. Somewhere in the back of
her mind she reserved the judgement that Neil Jardine

hadn't wanted her here and therefore intended to test her as hard as possible from the first moment, but she could submerge that and get on with the job. His manner didn't exactly suggest it anyway: he was impersonally efficient but helpful, showed her where everything was, and had both of them organised with an impressive speed which still managed to give the appearance of being unhurried.

It was difficult to realise afterwards that within twenty minutes of her arrival at Achnabrae House she was in the air.

The helicopter landed like a giant insect on a pad on one of the lawns which she hadn't previously had time to notice. The two doctors loaded their equipment and climbed in: in Neil's case it was a flat case of surgical instruments and in Bethany's a medical bag with drugs, syringes, tubing, and anything else she might need. A package marked Sterile Theatre Pack had appeared from somewhere and there was also a small transportable anaesthesia kit which looked rather like the air-tanks used for scuba-diving. 'Rule one, take everything, in case!' Neil commented briefly; gave a thumbs-up to the pilot; and then pulled himself into the plastic bubble which made the helicopter's body and settled himself beside her.

It was noisy, with a deafening rattle which increased as they took off. Bethany couldn't put on the protective ear-muffs which hung on a hook on the fuselage beside her because Neil had begun a shouted running commentary on what they would find on the rig, where it was situated, and what a sea-based rig for oil or gas exploration looked like. If he had paused,

Bethany might have told him drily that she had seen them on television. Even while she was thinking so he broke off to exchange a few words with the pilot and she was able at last to look round. And down. Their rattling progress seemed to carry then remarkably quickly across the varying patterns of the landscape below, in a way which was almost dizzying.

'Don't look down when you're not used to it, you'll feel as if you're swinging on the end of a string and get vertigo,' Neil's voice commanded brusquely. He didn't give her time to answer, merely reached out a hand and jerked her chin firmly upwards to reinforce his words. Then he leaned forward to speak to the pilot again. It didn't seem to be anything to do with their destination, more like something in code—until she realised abruptly that they were actually having a shouted conversation about American football.

She was annoyed with Neil for giving her that curt command not to look down and even more annoyed by his gesture which seemed to leave a tingling along her jaw. He had been right, though. The fascination of seeing the land spread out below her like a map *had* been tinged with an uncertain feeling of disorientation which seemed to squeeze her stomach. When they came out over the sea, grey-green and choppy-looking, she deliberately kept her gaze straight ahead after one tiny glance downwards. It wasn't so interesting looking at empty sky, but it felt safer.

They began to hover and then to sink. Bethany took care not to look down, but she didn't shut her eyes either. It was weird but intriguing to find her eye-level view being gradually shut in by the giant matt grey shapes of pipework and girders. A television screen never showed the massive dwarfing scale of everything.

They were met by a tough-looking character in a hard hat and overalls. He greeted Neil easily if with a touch of apology for the need to call him out, but Bethany was aware of a flash of surprise in his eyes for her. Neil introduced her casually as Dr Dale with absolutely no reference to her gender and then they were being taken below. Once inside it felt so much like a ship that it was hard to remember they were in a fixed structure. They were shown rapidly along various narrow corridors until they reached an obviously well equipped medical suite.

A patient was a patient anywhere. Bethany snapped into feeling at home with remarkable ease. The medical suite boasted a portable X-ray and film from two angles was already available. Three fractured metacarpal bones showed up, but there was no splintering. The owner of the injured hand was looking pale but resigned. He also looked very young and was obviously trying not to wince from the thought of having his fingers set. She was able to see, then, how Neil took trouble to put him at his ease by discussing the whole thing with him in easy and practical tones.

He decreed a light general anaesthetic without bothering to dress it up as consultation. Bethany had to remind herself that he was the boss, and that she was an unknown quantity to him, otherwise she might have been tempted to a dry comment once the patient was out. It occurred to her then, wryly, that she had been rather more used to working lately with registrars of her own level, not for someone intrinsically senior. She'd have to remember that.

Watching his economy of movement, his careful but easy skill, did give her a sense of approval and the knowledge that he knew exactly what he was doing. Neuro-surgery might be responsible for a lot of those impressive letters after his name, but he was obviously at home with lesser types of injury too.

It was only after they had taken off again, with a deafening rattle of noise and a swaying movement, that she came to herself enough to lean towards Neil with a necessary question.

'What will happen to him now?'

'He'll be flown off to convalesce, once the rig nurse is satisfied he's over any post shock. They'll get in touch with us again if there should be any problems —though I don't anticipate any.'

It was somehow disconcerting that he had leaned close to answer, which brought his lips inches from her cheek. With annoyance, Bethany crushed the sudden sense of his forceful masculinity that flashed involuntarily through her. She saw a glint of bright blue between lowered eyelids as he looked down at her, and sought quickly for something else to say.

'How do you land on one of those things if it's rough weather?'

'With difficulty. We may have to find out one of these days. By the way, you can give yourself a gold star for quick adaptation.'

He leaned away from her again and turned to look out at the sky before she could answer. There would be no way to regain his attention against the steady rattle and thump of the engine short of pinching the strong muscular arm which lay close to her own. She felt a sudden intense awareness of its presence there, which seemed to send magnetic quivers through her padded jacket. She switched her mind sharply away with a quick annoyance.

It was tempting to catch condescension in his approving remark. Then, with a grin, she relaxed and took pleasure in it instead. None of this afternoon felt quite real yet, but she could certainly feel a glow of triumph. She had come through a first test to everyone's satisfaction, including her own.

And Neil Jardine had been there to notice.

He didn't offer any more conversation, and after a grinding half-hour they were coming in to land on the green lawns of Achnabrae House. Bethany did look down as they came in, this time. She told herself she was used to it now and she wanted to see how the Manor looked from the air. This view-point showed its dominant isolation amongst the rolling scenery of moor and hill, with the windbreak screen of pines to one side and a scattering of small trees forming another protection to the rear. From up here, Bethany could just catch the metallic glint of a whiplash-slender radio mast rising from the roofs towards the rear.

They sank smoothly and steadily, and then they were down. The chopper pilot brought them in to touch ground as lightly as a descending leaf, with the same casual professionalism he had shown all afternoon. He turned to give them a thumbs-up as they climbed out, the face beneath his helmet young and cheerful. Then they were moving away at a crouch to keep them low under the down-draught of the rotor, whose buffet made Bethany feel both blown and deafened.

She couldn't resist turning to watch as their gleaming bird of passage lifted slowly and tidily into the air again and moved away like some futuristic but friendly dragonfly. It gave her a sense of wonder to think that she would soon be thoroughly used to it. For now, it was still an enthralling sight to send a quiver of sheer fascination along her nerves.

Next time, however, she would know how to jump out quickly and not need a steadying hand under her elbow. She was annoyed with herself for the hesitation that must have made Neil reach for her with one strong well-shaped hand; and for the instant awareness it gave her of his strength. She would have to make it clear that small and slight she might be, but she was as tough as any of them——

Excitement suddenly came back, with the half-disbelieving knowledge that she was actually here, already doing the job which had occupied so much of her thoughts for the past few weeks. Her mouth began to curve into a smile of pleasure. If everyone back at the hospital could see her now!

A deep voice spoke behind her with a tinge of humour in it, breaking into her thoughts. 'Now, I guess, I'll actually give you the time to unpack and settle in. There's your car where you left it, so I'll even give you a hand to bring in your luggage!'

'There's no need,' Bethany said promptly.

'Don't spoil your excellence by standing on your

dignity. I fought to have you here, against a good many objections, and ruffling up against normal civility is merely stupid!'

Bethany decided to ignore the last abrasive remark for the time being. Her brown eyes had widened as they flew to his face.

'You fought to have me here?' she repeated disbelievingly. 'Why?'

'Because of your qualifications,' he said drily, as if her accusing tone had suggested something else. 'Firstly, I wanted a second anaesthetist and they didn't want to give me one. Secondly, your background experience: if it did come up that we needed another surgeon in an emergency you're qualified even if out of practice. And thirdly, you seemed eminently suitable for the type of work. I may have put you into the interviews on impulse and to add a bit of extra competition, but when I tried out your ability to think on your feet without preparation you came through with flying colours!'

'Thanks!'

'No thanks needed. I made it deliberately tough and you had the courage of your convictions, that's all!'

It seemed clear the she had squeaked into the job by the skin of her teeth. Telling her so didn't seem designed to increase her confidence, and she regarded him with a lift of her chin.

'You said ''against a good many objections''—whose?'

'Mainly, our revered company president, whose particular baby this accident unit is.'

'*Mr Travis* objected to me? That wasn't how it

seemed at the interview!'

'Oh, you were taken in by his soft-spoken manner, were you? You should be warned—his immediate staff call him the Great Piranha behind his back! He's as tough as tensile steel, that one, and he likes things done *his* way!'

Bethany's experience so far, and a glint in the sapphire blue eyes, put it on to the tip of her tongue to suggest that Mr Travis wasn't alone in that. However, Neil was going on.

'He doesn't actually go in for employing women when he can help it, however much he may pay lip-service to the idea. In this case he did have a point in feeling that your presence might cause problems—but as you happened to have exactly the qualifications I needed, I got my way. Now, for goodness' sake, let's get that car of yours unpacked and go indoors!'

'Wait a minute. What was that about my causing problems? I'd just like to know why *you* think——'

He had turned to stride towards her small scarlet car, still standing where she had left it, so that she had to trail after him on the words. He was waiting for her to unlock the boot and she reached for the keys still tucked into her trouser pocket. Her half-uttered question made him glance at her with one black eyebrow raised.

'Site work's very much a man's world, whether you like it or not. Still, we'll get over that, if only by ignoring it—like today—and giving them the chance to get used to you. But I surely don't need to make the point about your living here?'

'You'd better go ahead and make it!'

'All right. Since you *are* rather noticeably feminine, you might bear in mind the complications it could cause. We'll all work better without emotional distractions—so don't go and fall for anyone, or encourage anyone to fall for you!'

'Of all the incredibly chauvinist remarks——' The words came out in a splutter. Neil had reached over to lift the car keys out of her hand and was now calmly opening her car boot. Bethany found her voice again.

'Do *all* the females around here act as objects of your suspicion? I mean, surely I can't be the only one to spoil the monastic atmosphere? Or have you already issued a general instruction—put up a notice in the village shop perhaps——'

A gleam of amusement came into his eye. 'It hasn't occurred to me so far. I suspect the locals will look on us as alien strangers and leave us alone, and I wouldn't want to put ideas into their heads, would I?'

'Then I'm surprised you aren't afraid you've put then into mine! Goodness, what an opportunity for me, surrounded by a glamorous selection of hungry males!' Bethany dropped sarcasm abruptly to give him a withering look. 'I've come here to work, as it happens, and that's *all* I intend to do! Imagining that what all women want most is a love affair—no matter *what else* they may be doing—isn't just male chauvinism, it's a good example of masculine conceit!'

Her infuriated acidity set him laughing outright this time. His head went back on the column of his throat and his eyes made sparkling blue slits.

'All right, touché! As long as we all know where we

stand.' He sobered abruptly and gave her a friendly look which, for some reason, sent an odd shock right through to her bones. 'I'm only bearing human nature in mind, and so, I suggest, should you. OK?'

He handed her back her car keys, lifted two suitcases as if they were featherlight, and strode away with them. His departure gave him the last word, and Bethany gazed after him with an exasperated resentment.

It was tinged with a bitter amusement suddenly. It certainly made a change to be seen as a possible femme fatale—after living with a man who found her so boring that he strayed, repeatedly, while she remained innocently trusting.

That gave her absolutely no reason to be caught by the knowledge that Neil Jardine was extremely attractive when he laughed.

She ducked her head in annoyance and reached down quickly to disentangle the rest of her luggage from its squashed condition in the bottom of her boot. Bother the man—and did he really think she wasn't *used* to working with men, after all her hospital years?

CHAPTER FIVE

SHE WENT into the house and was met by a small-statured, dark-eyed man who was waiting for her in the hall. He seemed to be some kind of general factotum, from the way he gave her a shy nod of his head and indicated that she was to follow him. In a softly-accented voice he said he would show her to her living quarters.

Her flatlet was on the second floor. It was pleasant if impersonal; a bedsitting-room with bathroom and toilet ensuite and a miniature kitchen area with a small fridge and an electric kettle. The furniture was light pine and there was a bookcase and desk in one corner, a television set incorporated neatly on a rotating shelf, and one of the ubiquitous internal telephones attached to the wall beside the bed. The two suitcases Neil had brought in were sitting in the middle of the floor, but there was no other sign of him.

Looking round, Bethany was reminded of the living accommodation offered in conference centres; but the neat and well-arranged space would have covered both the main rooms of the small flat she and Daniel had shared.

She wasn't going to think of Daniel. Nor, after what she had just said to Neil, was she going to remember how easy it was to be vulnerable to emotion even in the middle of a work situation. Perhaps even more, then, under the pressures which built up—if the right two people happened to find themselves thrown together . . .

The view from her window drew her and she went to lean her hands on the sill. This wasn't the same impressive sweep of scenery she had seen from the front of the house, but she decided she liked it almost better. There was a fairy-tale quality in looking down at a small walled kitchen garden, and then beyond that a gentle dropping away of moorland with distant pines marching in from the left. They cut off the horizon in a blue-green blur, with ruler-straight lines making the shadows beneath like the child's drawing of a wood. Bethany drew a deep breath of appreciation. Whatever else happened here, *this* was both a luxury and an enchantment.

Later, she ventured forth to familiarise herself with the rest of the house. Peter Llewellyn appeared while she was hesitating in the hall and offered to show her round. As they did the tour she began to feel that the Manor had been turned into a cross between a hotel and a high-tech nursing home without any beds. The front of the house with its living quarters, communal dining and sitting-rooms, and even a small well-equipped gymnasium, had all the comfort of a well-thought-out residential hotel, but the back was full of medical store-rooms, electronically-run autoclave equipment, computer link-ups, and, of course, the radio room. This was full of gleaming equipment

Bethany hadn't a hope of recognising, and as a dominant feature there was a large computerised wall-map with FTI sites marked by symbols.

'It looks almost terrifyingly efficient——'

'It is, isn't it, Dave?' The young man thus addressed was manning the board, and had just shown Bethany how, when there was a call-out, lights would flash into place to show who had gone where. 'They do seem to have thought of everything! Come on, I'll show you Neil's office. It's just round the corner from here.'

Bethany stiffened a little at the thought that he would find her going round with Peter—though if he drew conclusions that she was trying to charm him, she thought drily, he'd be wrong. Her co-anaesthetist seemed the quiet type and certainly not the sort to throw out any sexual challenges. When they reached Neil's office, however, it was empty. It seemed oddly impersonal. There was a similar wall-map to the one in the radio room, a computer link-up and VDU, telephones, filing cabinets, and a large desk—but no personal clutter lying about, not even a favourite well-thumbed surgical textbook. The only thing she could conclude from it was that he was tidy and well organised.

Over the next few days, Bethany found herself with a remarkable amount of time on her hands. She wasn't required to make a return visit to Rig Two. She wasn't called out to anywhere else either, though Erik was sent on what was apparently an exploratory visit to one of the other rigs. It was strange to have so little to do, after the constant rush of hospital work. She spent much of her time withdrawing to the privacy of her flat, just to make sure that no one thought she was hanging about asking for attention.

She did meet the others over communal meals in the pleasant dining-room, which gave her a chance to establish a brisk no-nonsense manner and an air of deliberately sexless civility.

It had occurred to her unwillingly that Neil did have a point, when she discovered that apart from Mrs Vasquez who was half of the Filipino couple who ran the house, she *was* the only female resident here. There was a Vasquez baby of about eighteen months, though it was kept firmly out of sight and, she gathered, even that was a boy. The cleaning was done by an outside firm whose male operatives arrived in a van twice a week from forty miles away. Perhaps it wasn't altogether surprising that Bethany could sense an initial wariness in the atmosphere whenever she appeared.

It eased. Lang, who had struck Bethany as distinctly watchful and inclined to throw out challenges, calmed down after Bethany had ignored a couple of spiked invitations to argument, and began addressing her in a more casual and relaxed fashion. After a call had come in which took the two of them to another minor rig injury he seemed to accept that she wasn't going to expect special treatment. Peter went on being easy and quiet, though Bethany had the impression that his placid manner actually concealed a nervous temperament. As for Erik, he never showed any

signs of knowing Bethany was female at all: he
treated everyone in exactly the same sunny manner.
She thought with some amusement that, consider-
ing he was very handsome in his own giant way, it
must be a disappointment to half the human race
to find that he reserved his most passionate interest
for keeping fit.

'He's crazy,' Lang commented as the giant
young Swede emerged from an energetic session in
the gymnasium to do a mile run before having
breakfast.

'But cheerful with it.' Peter suggested good
humouredly.

'Oh yes, I'll grant you that. He doesn't even
mind being told he's crazy. He just says, "It's good
to be fit, ho?" and thunders off to do another
thousand press-ups!'

Lang's lugubrious expression made Bethany
chuckle. 'The only thing he misses here is a
swimming pool, he says. Pity we haven't got an icy
loch, or he could thrash up and down it at high
speed!'

'Heaven preserve us, it's like living with an
oversized sheepdog without having him wet as
well! I just hope his endless energy doesn't give
Neil ideas. Can't you imagine him deciding to line
us all up on the lawn for physical jerks, like the
staff in a Japanese factory?' Lang glanced round
as the door opened on his speech and offered their
arriving chief of surgery a look between ruefulness
and amusement. 'No, *don't* go and tell me that's a
good idea!'

'As I know you're not as idle as you pretend to be, I won't take you up on it. Sessions in the gym aren't a bad idea, though. That's what it's there for,' Neil came round the table with an easy grace and pulled out a chair beside Bethany.

She had known he was there without turning her head. However much she took care not to show it, an awareness of him seemed to permeate her nerves whenever he was near at hand. She found all at once that he was addressing her.

'There's a query grumbling appendix on one of the rigs. You can fly over and have a look at it later. Just a diagnostic visit, it doesn't sound like anything that'll need dealing with in situ——'

'Oh, right, I'll get ready!'

'No rush, you can finish your breakfast.' A hand restrained her from rising and she had to still an immediate consciousness of its firmness against her bare forearm. 'Tell Dave or Johnny when you're ready to go and they'll call for a pilot,' Neil added calmly in a voice which made her feel, with annoyance, that he thought she needed soothing for her jumpiness.

'There doesn't seem to be much happening at the moment,' Lang put in, making it half a question.

'No, they're still getting used to the idea that we're available. Don't tempt providence or they'll have a series of accidents all at once!'

When Bethany left them a few minutes later they were discussing a multiple accident situation Lang had once been involved with, talking shop as surgeons always seemed to do even over meals. She had pricked her ears unconsciously to see if Neil would give away anything about himself. He seemed singularly capable of silence about his past. By now she knew bits and pieces about Lang's life, and his New Zealand background, and that he laid claim to having several air-hostess girlfriends who definitely took second place to his ruling passion for fast cars; she knew that Peter, so far from being Welsh, was actually half German, and that Erik came from a large farming family; just as they knew about her that her parents lived in Australia to which they had happily emigrated while she was in medical school. But about Neil she knew virtually nothing. She had heard him mention in passing that he'd spent some time working in Canada, but apart from that she knew no more concrete facts than she had when she came here.

Only what she could observe: that he ran things with an air of practical efficiency, that he was self-contained, and that it was impossible to be near him without being aware of the reined-in force of his temperament.

He might handle his position here with a deceptive casualness, but he also made sure his leadership was unquestioned. The merest lift of a black eyebrow was enough to ensure that. A cartoon of him, she thought drily, would probably put him in jackboots with a whip . . .

To be fair, the other men obviously liked him and respected his judgement. *They* didn't seem to feel any curiosity as to why he was here throwing his energies into running a small private accident service set in remote surroundings—when he might surely have been a rising star somewhere else.

He certainly wouldn't have met the kind of obstructions she had in *her* career. For that matter, at thirty-five why wasn't he married? He could surely have had his pick there too . . . and men were never asked to make a choice between marriage and a career, with the question coming up at every job interview!

Except of course here, Bethany remembered with a touch of dry irony.

She made her way to the radio room with a smile of ironic amusement curving her lips. Neil certainly needn't have worried about the radio boys. As far as she could see they had an average age of about twenty-two, and she wasn't their type anyway, to judge from the page three pin-ups they seemed to favour. The pilots lived out and led their own highly detached lives, so that took care of them, and she imagined Neil must have seen by now that she wasn't going to endanger the concentration of her team of colleagues. He could really have saved himself the trouble of making his lordly comments.

She certainly wasn't going to be swept by an annoying, half-wistful knowledge that the only person here who drew her with a disturbing sense of attraction, and curiosity, and physical magnetism, was him.

It was illogical, when her nights were broken all too often with memories of Daniel. Now that she no longer fell into bed bleary with tiredness there was all too much chance for her body to come alive with the rememberance of his touch. She could tell herself angrily that it was habit, that it would pass. It was certainly no cure to find her mind drifting to contemplate a certain dark, lean, athletic form instead, to visualise the challenging gaze of a pair of sapphire eyes as vividly blue as a Siamese cat's.

It was *definitely* no cure, but a distraction, when she had to meet those same eyes across the breakfast table, and respond to an amiable 'Good morning' uttered in a deep, slightly abrasive voice!

She flew out to the same rig she had gone to on her first day, and found the rig foreman accepting her simply as 'the doc' now that she was becoming a familar figure. It was like a standard casualty call to be testing for an inflamed appendix and she was fairly sure it was only persistent constipation, but told them to radio in again if there were further worries. Two days later she was sent to another rig to look at a case of swollen glands, and a day after that she and Lang made the longer journey to the northernmost rig to set a broken arm. Bethany began to feel she was never going to do anything but sea-based minor accidents —and, almost, that Neil would deliberately keep her to them, from the way he chose to discuss the other sites with Peter.

Perhaps she was ungrateful to think so. It surely ought to be exciting enough to flit to and fro in helicopters so often.

He and Peter took the job when a call came in from Alaska to a drilling accident. They were gone a week. Nothing else came in during their absence. Lang passed the time by jacking up his Lamborghini and lovingly oiling parts of its engine. Erik pounded about in shorts and track-shoes or could be seen expanding his vast chest in breathing exercises; and Bethany felt a restless longing to explore the nearer moors but knew she couldn't in case an emergency call came in. There were certain frustrations about the job she hadn't counted on. She was almost inclined to wish she was back at the hospital, with the familiarity of plenty to do instead of too much time to think.

It was rather late for that, just as it was too late for her night-time thoughts which persistently made her wonder what Daniel was doing—whether he was happy— whether he might even have decided to miss her——No, probably not that; he would have angrily abandoned all thoughts of her now that she had involved herself in private work.

It was odd, she thought with a touch of bitterness, that he could combine political principle with unprincipled charm. Anyway, she was finished with all that—with letting *any* man disturb her thoughts!

Neil came back looking tired and roughened with tension. The following day he seemed to have recovered and snapped commandingly at the end of breakfast, 'Bethany, you'd better go and do a round of the rigs again just to see how they're doing—get the radio room to set it up!'

'The slave-driver finds work for idle hands to do . . .' Lang murmured half under his breath—though carefully after Neil had left the room. He glanced at Bethany. 'At least for yours!'

'He's been having a fret because we're under-used,' Peter put in, his tone peaceable. 'Apparently there was originally an idea that one team should do regular rounds to the further sites as well, but now head office has decided not carry that through.'

'That does rather keep us on ice, doesn't it? Oh well, let's not knock it—*I* don't mind being paid to do damn all!'

'Pity we aren't near enough to cover their South American sites from here. Still I'd imagine they're working on that one for later—if *we* prove useful.'

'How was Alaska, anyway?' Lang asked as Bethany moved to call the radio room and request a helicopter and a warning to the rigs.

'A bit of a nasty one. Needed a mid-thigh amputation.' That would make it heavy on the anaesthetics side, Bethany reflected, listening as Peter answered. 'We made an arrangement with the American air-base hospital for post-op care. They seem to be pretty efficient, so we didn't need to hang around for the follow-up.'

Then the emergency team had been able to return in the waiting company jet, Bethany knew. She felt a touch of envy, because it was a form of transport she hadn't experienced yet. She'd also like to have seen Neil operating . . .

She'd begun to wonder whether she ever would, with Peter definitely in the position of senior anaesthetist. It was two weeks later when the internal phone beside her bed gave a sharp insistent buzz at six a.m. A moment later Neil's voice was telling her curtly to get ready to leave for an emergency in Greenland.

CHAPTER SIX

WHEN BETHANY heard it was spinal injuries she had
expected to be going with Neil, but when she emerged
into the cool and faintly misty morning with her
collection of equipment to hand he was there without
his flying gear and was briefing Erik. The helicopter
had already landed and was waiting for them. There
was only time to notice that Neil gave her a brief
frowning look and that he double checked her
equipment, before they were taking off. Bethany
hoped the nerves that clenched her stomach didn't
show.

Afterwards, the time they spent getting there had
almost vanished from her mind, though at the time it
seemed like an endless and unreal suspension. First
there was the helicopter transit, squashed up against
Erik who took up a predictable amount of room; then
a hasty crossing of tarmac to a small waiting private
jet, with their leaving formalities apparently pre-
cleared. They were in the air again without delay, and
Bethany tried to ignore the fact that they were tearing
through the sky at high speed as she listened to Erik
passing on what was known about the accident. It
sounded like a bad one: only one injured, but that one
in a severe enough condition to make her instinctively
wince.

The accident had happened in a difficult place to
reach, too, so they had barely landed when they

66

were off in another helicopter. That wasn't all. A jeep waited for them after this landing and they had another half-hour of bumpy travel along a rough half-made road through jagged rocky terrain. The route was ringed with icy mountains and the sun blazed from a high bleached sky—but cold air tore at the lungs and bit through gloved fingers.

Their destination was on a rock-strewn slope with only a partially-cleared space round it. In the clear light Bethany could see the heavy gouge where a massive digger had slid and overturned. Somehow, the machine had been lifted and moved away; but behind the canvas screens which had been erected to make a shelter must be the man who had been trapped underneath the crushing weight of the huge vehicle . . .

Afterwards, again, Bethany couldn't remember whether there had been surprise at the sight of her slight feminine figure in any of the set faces of the men who hurried her and Erik across to the shelter. Only relief, she thought, as hands reached out to carry anything that might be heavy. Then she was following Erik as he strode ahead putting quick questions and receiving equally rapid answers; and in a moment they were able to see and assess their patient.

She had known Erik must be good to be offered the FTI job. Now, suddenly, she found out just how good. He didn't seem to turn a hair at the injuries which had prevented the man's being moved at all, nor at the primitive conditions around him; and when he looked at Bethany and said in a determined voice, 'We shall mend what we can, and see,' she could tell by the look in his eyes that he didn't intend to be daunted by the impossible. Which he then proceeded to perform.

They could really have done with two surgeons. However, the anaesthesia was tricky enough to take up all Bethany's time. More than once she thought they would lose their patient, but Erik operated on with delicacy and intelligence. He was only, he explained calmly as he worked, going to do enough to allow transit away from here in a specially-constructed cradle for which he had already issued instructions. Just so much to relieve the pressure here, give support there, avoid a sudden break-out of internal bleeding . . .

It seemed unlikely that they would manage to move someone in this state of shock and trauma along the rough road to the nearest helicopter landing base, but they did. It seemed incredible that he could be moved on from there in a strapped-on stretcher without fatality, but he was. Then, at a properly-equipped hospital at last, Bethany could begin to relax—but not Erik, who promptly went into a huddle with the resident surgeons. Not long afterwards they were back in a proper theatre in borrowed gowns to continue with the more urgent repair work.

It was undeniable that Erik's combination of undimmed faith and extreme skill had saved the man's life. The tension didn't seem to affect him, either. When they finally caught the jet on the first leg of their journey back to Achnabrae he stretched heartily, gave Bethany a grin, and then promptly went to sleep with the immediacy of a child.

She was too keyed up to sleep herself and was conscious of a bone-deep weariness when the helicopter set them down on Achnabrae's lawns. She was almost in a trance as they made their way in through the side door, logged in at the radio room, and were told that Neil was in his office waiting for a full report. Meeting the blue eyes and seeing that they held nothing but an impersonal assessment of the situation described to him gave Bethany a flash of resentment—but Erik was going on to add a generous note of praise.

'This is one very good anaesthetist we have here, I may tell you, Neil! Without Bet'anee, I could not have managed so much!'

'Really? Well, you're both due a couple of days off shift now. Let me have a proper taped report of everything for the records during that time.' His lack of reaction struck Bethany like a slap in the face. Then he made it worse by going on, 'I'm glad it worked out, when I couldn't send Pete with you. And congratulations on achieving so much, too. I was afraid it sounded like a hopeless one, from what they said when they called in the emergency!'

'Oh, not so bad as give up. This time we win, ho? Now I go and shower and exercise—I sleep on the plane and I feel frowsty!'

Erik left cheerfully, but Bethany lingered. Tiredness lowered her defenses and brought an anger she tried to hide as she asked levelly,

'Just as a matter of record, do I gather you would have sent Pete rather than me, for preference? Do you mind telling me why?'

'Because he has more rough-conditions experience. Anyway, I'd have aimed to take you on your first major accident myself.'

'Then why didn't you? You could have taken the case!'

'You're querying my decisions rather thoroughly this morning!' The unwavering blue stare was frosty for a moment, but then relaxed into a tolerance which was almost more maddening. 'You're still strung up, aren't you? You obviously did well, so let's forget it. If you like I'll say you did *very* well; clearly, from the fact that what we all hate most didn't happen, and you didn't lose the patient during surgery!'

'Did you expect I would? Then I'm surprised you sent me out at all!'

'You're suffering from reaction.' Neil had been standing behind his desk while Bethany faced him across it with her eyes flashing angrily, and now he moved round it to seize hold of both her elbows and give her a little shake. 'Come on, Bethany, pull yourself together and go and get some rest. You did very well and I'm pleased with you, OK?'

'I wasn't asking for a pat on the head, thanks. In my book all the credit goes to Erik.' With that she detached herself from him and turned on her heel and left him.

Emotion was clogging her throat, but she couldn't afford tears. It was bad enough to have him take hold of her as if she needed soothing like a child. Anger, and a sudden distasteful suspicion, had almost made her snap back at him. Was the reason he hadn't gone himself, when he was the obvious person with all his neuro-surgical qualifications, the fact that he'd judged the case as hopeless—and didn't want a failure on *his* record?

She'd known consultants like that.

She didn't want to think it about Neil. It would be like finding out that someone her instincts drew her to admire had feet of clay. The query stayed in her mind to dog her thoughts. It wasn't that *anyone* could have done better than Erik, who had gone up several notches in her estimation; it was just a matter of principle and responsibility. A blow to her own ability to judge character too—or, she wondered bitterly, was she simply letting attraction cloud her judgement yet again?

It wasn't an attraction she wanted to feel, in any case. It simply nagged her, and set her at odds with herself. There was something about Neil's self-contained manner which acted as an irritant, just as his physical presence sharpened her always into awareness of him. Too often, over pleasant discussions during meals, she would catch herself out in a desire to compete for his attention—and in the general comments he did make, there was almost always a sense that he and she thought the same way . . . She would resist it, but the knowledge made her give a sharp sigh when she was alone.

Erik's tirelessness had given her food for thought, like a nudge to remind her that she had always been proud of her own stamina. It would be all too easy to go soft under working conditions which had long spells of inactivity in between and a fitness programme suddenly didn't seem such a bad idea. One morning a week after they had returned from Greenland she made her way down to the gym dressed in brief shorts and a sleeveless T-shirt, determined to work herself into shape.

She had chosen a time when she had seen Lang going out towards the garages, but she was prepared to face him out if he suddenly came back and made some of his mocking comments. The square room with its gleaming equipment was empty, so she didn't have to cope with Erik's enthusiastic approval either, which gave her a sense of relief. She looked round and then chose an exercise bike and set herself to some arduous pedalling.

There was quite a variety of equipment to try. A quarter of an hour later she was lying on her back on the floor doing pull-ups against a spring-loaded bar, feeling the stretch in her leg muscles. She'd probably done about enough . . .

The door opened. From upside-down Bethany saw pale blue tracksuited legs, a lean wide-shouldered torso in a navy singlet which emphasised the smooth muscular gleam of skin, and then the firm planes of a face thrown into strange angles by this unfamiliar viewpoint. The sapphire eyes and black hair were unmistakable, however; and so was the deep voice which greeted her amiably.

'Someone else with the same idea? No, don't stop, there's plenty of room in here for both of us!'

Bethany's hands automatically let go of the spring and it bounced against the bar with a sharp clatter. She decided abruptly that she would feel more like herself right way up. She scrambled quickly to her feet with an unexpected unsteadiness and found herself being watched judically.

'You came up too fast from that one. Try some slow breathing and then a balance exercise to counter it. Go on—oh, and don't try to do too much all in one go, when you're not used to it!'

'I'll have to get Erik to give me some advice,' Bethany responded sweetly; and then wondered whether her voice, coming out with a gruff breathlessness, had sounded as ungracious to Neil as it did in her own ears. She tried not to feel riveted as he swung himself up easily on to some parallel bars, balancing gracefully against the strength of his forearms. She made herself stand still and start taking slow regular breaths, but it was difficult not to watch him out of the corner of her eye.

'I thought dance was the most fashionable exercise for women,' Neil said conversationally, apparently able to control his breathing enough to talk as well as exercise.

'Did you? I've never had time to take it up. I think I'll go now——'

'Stay and finish your breathing exercises or I'll think I've frightened you away.'

There seemed to be a mocking note under the remark. Bethany decided to ignore it: she also decided, abruptly, that she would continue exercising. She was just as much entitled to be in here as he was, and there was a set of simplified yoga exercises she'd once learned which would serve as a demonstration that she didn't need his advice.

There was a silence for several moments, but it was difficult to concentrate against her awareness of the man across the room, all smooth muscle and lightly-bronzed shoulders, his back view giving her the sight of narrow waist and lean hips and healthy, athletic maleness.

He swung down from the bars and Bethany ducked her head quickly, trying to make it look part of the exercise she was doing. She would do one more arm and leg lift from her seated position and then she would definitely stop. She tried to ignore the view she had of Neil's tracksuited legs crossing the room towards the rowing machine, and came smoothly to her feet, reaching for the towel she had brought down with her and slinging it round her neck.

'Going? You know, you're giving me a distinctly frosty feeling. You wouldn't by any chance still be sulking because I mentioned that I'd have sent Peter out instead of you if he hadn't been laid up with a stomach upset?'

Bethany's head jerked round with such rapidity that she could almost feel her neck crack. Neil was standing watching her with his eyebrows raised, and she met a disconcerting challenge in the blue eyes steadily regarding her.

'Certainly not, I never sulk. Do you have to——'

'*Something* seems to be the matter. So tell me what it is!'

Bethany drew a breath. His directness was disconcerting. 'All right,' she said, her chin lifting as she gave him a straight look in return. 'It's actually nothing but idle curiosity, but why *didn't* you go to Greenland yourself? You knew it was a spinal, and you're the one with the specialised experience!'

A glimmer of surprise showed in his eyes. 'Obvious,

surely? If another emergency case came in while you were gone, someone would have to take it without a fully-trained anaesthetist, since Peter was off sick. Better if that's the most senior person—me. There's also the fact that I judged Erik would have the best chance with that kind of case, and a good temperament for handling it too. I don't really know why I should explain, but if you find it so important——'

'I told you it was just curiosity.' There was a sudden relief running through her, and an abrupt sense of humility too because his explanation was so reasonable. She gave him a quick, brilliant smile and a touch of apology in it. 'Sorry. I—I hadn't thought it through properly, so it was puzzling me. A specialist in neuro-surgery and a neuro-surgical case seemed to fit together!'

'As you seemed to have looked me up, didn't you notice my experience dated back a bit? I've been doing general work for the last few years.' There was a tightness about Neil's mouth as he spoke. Then he seemed to shrug off whatever tensions Bethany's words had caused him, and gave her a dry look. 'What were you mentally accusing me of—laziness? I've been called quite a few things, but idleness isn't *usually* counted as one of my faults! On the contrary,' he added, a reminiscent smile suddenly curling the narrow lips, 'one of my friends once offered to put me on a mental regimen to cure me of my "restless inner tension"!'

His expression made Bethany chuckle. 'Goodness, what was the friend, a Buddhist?'

'No, an Inuit. Canadian Eskimo to you,' Neil added as he saw her puzzled stare. 'Inuit simply means "the people" in their language, and it's what they choose to call themselves in preference to what someone else once christened them!'

'Oh. I don't really know anything about Eskimos —sorry, Inuit!'

'No, most people don't, unless they've worked up in the Arctic. There's a persistent view that they're simple primitives. In fact they've a strong culture of their own, but their civilisation seems alien to outsiders because it's all based on living above the tree-line. They've got about six different languages and a complex set of legends . . . and they're people to like and respect.'

He was smiling, his eyes looking into some far distance. Bethany looked at him curiously, with an urge to prompt him now that he was in this suddenly revelatory mood.

"Above the tree-line"? Is that where you worked? I did notice that there didn't seem to be any trees in Greenland!'

'Too much ice that far north for them to grow. Have you ever noticed how many of *our* images talk about trees? "Tree of Life", "Tree of Knowledge" . . . It's not surprising that the early settlers and the Eskimo found each other difficult to understand! Imagine a language with dozens of different words for snow in its different states, but none for wood—or for fruit!' Neil snapped out of memories abruptly, to Bethany's disappointment, and was suddenly regarding her again with a thoughtful and sharply alert gaze. 'I seem to have got off the point, which is why it mattered to you whether I did or didn't go to

Greenland. Unless of course you just have an urge to take over the administration?'

'I don't.' It was a pity he had gone back to that dry tone, and Bethany gave him a quick rueful smile and a shrug of her shoulders to indicate apology. 'Maybe I'm still getting used to having too much time to think——'

'That applies to all of us. Being an experimental set-up had its disadvantages.' He frowned for a moment, and she felt he was studying her face as if it were a stranger's whose details he was committing to memory. There was something in his look which sent a tingle running along her nerves, an unwary disturbance like the field of an electrical storm. When he went on it was with a sudden wariness, a hint of challenge.

'You seem to have been on the look-out for something to criticise, anyway. Time alone doesn't explain that, does it? Why, I wonder, do you choose to treat me as an enemy?'

'I don't! If anything, I'm always aware that *you're* waiting to criticise *me!*'

'Am I? Are you sure? Or is it just that there's something about you and me which seems to set the sparks flying whether we like it or not?'

The words held a hint of roughness in their depths, and even across the room they seemed to set up magnetism which vibrated through the air. It was almost like an acknowledgment that she disturbed his peace of mind in the same way that he disturbed hers. Bethany gulped and tumbled into speech.

'You chose to employ me——'

'So I did. And you were so sure you wouldn't be a disruption!' Neil said that with a wryness that made her catch her breath and sent a sudden prickling all along her skin.

'I—I'm not——'

'Let's say it's just the circumstances in which we find ourselves. Let's remember too that behind all this we have two quite separate lives.' Whatever it was he might have been showing, he had himself reined in now. Bethany felt a sharp stab of regret—and a consciousness of every line of his body as he stood poised and still, of the taut maleness of it, the firmly-muscled shoulders and the athletic thighs, the vibrant blackness of his hair which was echoed by a small vee of black curls showing above the line of his singlet. Then, abruptly, she was aware that his eyes had changed their expression to an amused, mocking coolness.

'You know, looking at you now you could be a twelve-year-old, with your tousled hair and in those clothes! If I hadn't known you were twenty-nine and a competent anaesthetist I'd never have guessed!'

'Thanks! Flat-chested and pre-pubertal and no danger to anyone—I trust!'

Neil let out a sharp breath and took one step towards her. Only one step, the movement halted almost as soon as it had begun. Bethany was caught by a sureness that he had meant to reach for her. The inner vision of his hands coming down hard on her shoulders brought a shivering knowledge of their strength and the warmth they would send burning through her. Then he was speaking again, in a tightly-controlled voice.

'Your description, not mine, though if you like it that way . . . But if we weren't here to work, throwing out challenges like that might get you more than you bargained for! Human nature being what it is!'

Their eyes seemed to lock across the room. Bethany was suddenly deprived of breath. She felt as if she were drowning in sapphire depths which held a sudden flare of such naked longing that it was like an arrow piercing her. Every nerve in her body seemed to clamour to respond, and it was as if the acute stillness in the room had sucked away everything but this. That scorching gaze snapped every defence for both of them, and it would only take one word, one heart-beat . . .

Neil turned away in an abrupt movement and bent to fiddle with something on the rowing machine. The release was as sharp as the twang of a bowstring.

Bethany felt her muscle slump. There was a pulsing ache in her throat as air sighed back into her lungs. Then, before she had had time to collect herself, she saw that he had turned back to look at her—and that this time, his eyes were masked and impersonal. There was a rough edge to his voice, but otherwise it was cool and clipped and held nothing but curt practicality.

'As I said once, close-quarters living can notch up emotion unnecessarily. You and I will both have to learn not to jump down each other's throats at the least excuse. You're defensive about anything you take to be criticism, and I'm not always as tactful as I should be—agreed? So . . . in the interests of peace and quiet, we'll both have to work on it, won't we?'

He was saying something else under the reasonable

words, Bethany thought—and then wondered in sudden confusion whether that wasn't so, whether she had simply imagined it. Her voice came out huskily, but with a passable imitation of his coolness.

'That sounds all right to me. I'm all in favour of peace and quiet!'

It seemed ironic that the door should swing open on her words, bounding back on its hinges with a forceful energy. Erik stood there, a picture of massive cheerfulness, his face lighting up at the sight of company in his beloved gymnasium. He gave Bethany a beaming smile.

'Ah, Bet'anee, you too come to exercise? That's good! Oh, but there was a telephone call for you just now, I didn't know where you were, so I took a message and the person wants you to ring back!'

'Really? I wasn't expecting to hear from anyone. Who was it?'

'Someone calling from Glasgow, he said you know the number. A Dr Daniel McKinley.'

The sound of Daniel's name made her feel very suddenly as if she had been thumped in the stomach.

'Him again?' Neil's voice drawled. 'He seems persistent!' As Bethany's widened eyes flew to his face she saw that it seemed to have shuttered itself into cynicism. 'No, I'm not there to pass on messages, particularly not when they come in on my private line,' he informed her smoothly. 'I told him you were working—which happened to be true—and that if he must get hold of you he could always write. Erik, come and show me how to change this machine's rate-counter, will you? If I try to row at something *you've* set, I'll probably end with a heart attack!'

CHAPTER SEVEN

HALF AN HOUR later Bethany was ringing the path lab number with a stiff memory of its familiarity. The decision to do so had been taken after some hesitation and she'd forgotten today was Sunday until the duty technician told her so. He didn't seem to recognise her voice, which was some kind of comfort, and when told it was a personal call, recited the private number of the flat.

So Daniel had gone back to living there . . . with his new love? If so, the ease with which she'd been given the number when they weren't supposed to be handed out suggested he still wasn't dedicated to fidelity. In fact he was being even more blatant about it, if the whole Path Department knew his phone number was on free offer to any female voice.

The deliberate cynicism of the thought seemed to strengthen her. It wasn't difficult, after all, to sound crisp and cool when the receiver the other end was picked up after three rings, and she heard the number spoken in a well-known light tenor voice.

'Daniel? It's Bethany. I believe you've been trying to get hold of me?'

'Beth! I was hoping you *would* ring back, this time. When you didn't answer my last message——'

'Actually I didn't get it. I'm sorry to disturb your Sunday, but it occurred to me that you might have had a call from my parents or something. I only sent them off an airmail recently and they might not have got my change of address.'

'Oh dear, is that the only reason you've weakened?' He sounded rueful—and a lot less stilted than she did. 'I thought, the first time I rang, that saying I couldn't cut the music centre in half and did you want it might fetch you out of your corner. But if whoever it was didn't even pass it on . . .'

Bethany's breath seemed to be caught in her throat. *That* was the message he had left. She'd given him that music centre as a present—a highly expensive present for their first so-called anniversary. It was a memory which didn't help her state of mind. She was fighting to answer with something coolly unemotional when she found Daniel was speaking again.

'Actually you left some other stuff too—kitchen things, and that footstool we bought for a joke on holiday—Beth? You are still there, aren't you? You haven't rung off?'

'No, I'm still here. I'm sure your present— um—flatmate can find a use for the kitchenware, and——'

'I haven't got a present flatmate. I'm trying to make it up, darling. And say I'm sorry. I know I was an idiot and a bastard, and I haven't really any right to ask you to forgive me. But I'm asking just the same. Beth?'

'Yes? I mean *no*——'

'It's awful not being able to talk face to face. Can't you come down for a few days? I'm not running a car at the moment, so it'd be difficult to me to come up.

Anyway, the first time I rang I got the distinct impression they didn't encourage even phone calls, let alone visitors. Who *was* that I spoke to anyway?'

'The first time? My chief of surgery.'

'I know that note in your voice. Is he as grim as you make him sound?' Daniel said with caressing amusement. 'Shall I guess the type—superior, with a high opinion of himself and a pot-belly to match? You *would* go and work amongst the fleshpots, darling! What is it up there, anyway—a private clinic?'

If his voice hadn't been stirring too many confusing emotions in her Bethany would have choked at his description of Neil. She was briefly tempted to snap back with a more truthful picture—in fact, to stress Neil's attractions in glowing colours, to claim with deliberate coyness that they were 'the best of friends'——She swallowed hard and tried to answer steadily. 'It's not a clinic, it's an accident unit, and no, I don't think it'd be a good idea for you to visit. I—well, for one thing I never know if I'm going to be working. We're on more or less permanent accident call. Anyway, I—I don't want you up here, Daniel. We broke up because *you* wanted someone else, remember?'

'I split up with her almost as soon as you'd gone. Honey——'

'Oh? And the next one? And the one after that?' She could only cope with that note in his voice by getting angry. 'From all I gathered once my eyes were open, thingummyjig wasn't the first!'

'She was. You've only got to speak to someone around here for tongues to wag, you know that.' A tight, angry note was beginning to creep into Daniel's voice too now. 'I *could* get sick of so many of your friends thinking I wasn't good enough for you, too! I don't know what it was about that cliquey set-up, but I was always on the other side of the tracks with that surgeons' crowd of yours—until you and I joined up, and then they *half* accepted me! No, look, Beth, let's not quarrel about unnecessary things, right? I'm being straight with you, I love you, I want you, I want us to get together again!'

'I'm doing private work, and you said——'

'I know, I know! I don't approve, we both know that. We both know why you rushed off into it, too. I . . . I guess I'm hoping that you might have got tired of it now. I'll bet there's still a job here for you. Or we could go somewhere else, both of us. Honey, I *have* made the first move, so say you'll at least think about it!'

The pleading, caressing note in his voice was starting up all the old memories. She and Daniel when they first met; falling in love 'across a crowded room' as they joked afterwards; the magic of those early days when everything seemed tinged with a glitter of gold because he had chosen her and she had chosen him . . . It was unbelievable suddenly that it could ever have been over. He said, 'Beth?' softly, and she was jerked into visualising him: stretched out on the bed, probably, the telephone receiver snuggled against his ear, one smooth lock of fair hair tumbling untidily across his forehead.

'I—I don't know. I don't know if I could ever trust you again——'

'What about me trusting you? I don't know what you've been up to the last couple of months, do I? Whose was the fractured accent who answered the phone to me this morning, anyway? For all I know he's some stunning Nordic type who's stolen your heart from me!'

'He is—distinctly stunning, and about six foot five. I was on an accident with him a couple of days ago and he's a stunning surgeon too.' Bethany abruptly remembered Daniel's remark a moment ago about her 'surgeons' crowd' and a jealousy she'd never thought about for her more glamorous end of the profession. Could Daniel *really* have felt like that, felt excluded . . .? An unexpected guilt caught at her—but then all her doubts came rushing back too, muddling her, setting her rubbing her forehead with despairing fingers.

'I don't know what you want, Daniel. I haven't heard from you for months and then you throw this at me——'

'You do know what I want—I've just told you. There's been time for us both to cool off, think about things. I know you must be on a contract, but surely it's got a get-out clause? On, say marriage?'

'*Marriage*?'

'We might do better if we tied each other down. Don't you think?'

She couldn't think. His words didn't seem quite the right way of putting it, either. He was waiting for her to say something—and wasn't it what she'd always wanted? Daniel, marriage, a family—and before she got too old to have one, too, before chasing work turned her into someone who'd missed the chance of knowing what that other side of life?

'Well, I've said it, anyway,' Daniel's voice offered persuasively in her ear. 'You can't claim I haven't. Promise you'll think about it, darling? And listen, I swear I won't turn into one of those "woman-in-the-kitchen" types, or stop you working, or anything like that. I know you too well for that and I love you the way you are. I'm going to ring off now and leave you to brood. OK? And you know how to reach me. Just don't leave it too long—promise?'

'I—look, we haven't really discussed anything——'

'Yes, we have. I wish it didn't have to be over the phone when I'd rather be holding you. You know that, don't you? But get some time off and come down and see me—and see if you can say no to me then!'

Bethany heard him put the phone back very gently on its cradle. She heard the buzz in her ear as the line was freed and began its dialling purr. The small room in which she was standing—the little private study off the hall where the general-use outside telephone lvied—came slowly back into focus. Dazedly, she knew she must write down her call in the book—and then, above all, she must reach the total privacy of her flat.

The view from her room seemed strangely alien as she pushed up the window sash and stood taking deep dragging breaths of the clear warm air. It had turned summery over the last few days and the moors stretching out below the house seemed to glow with deep subtle colours. Bethany stared at them unseeingly.

Daniel . . . Daniel sorry, apologising, wanting her—wanting *marriage* . . .

Her thoughts seemed to tumble in confusion, thrown back by the sound of his voice into past memories. She tried to shake herself into sense. What about her job here?

Surely she couldn't back off now—and prove the truth of what everyone said about employing women!

The accident unit wouldn't exactly fall apart without her, though. She wouldn't even be leaving them short-staffed, in their present sporadic work pattern.

A sound below her made her look down. The Vasquez child was toddling happily round the kitchen garden, a dark-haired bundle on unsteady legs. Bethany's heart gave a sudden wistful squeeze. It was always the same, that need to be torn between heart and head; between herself as a doctor and herself as a woman . . .

She and Daniel had never discussed children. She had taken it for granted that her unspoken dreams were shared. But just now he'd said, 'I won't stop you working, I know you too well for that,' as if work was always going to be the only thing she wanted. Besides him. Maybe he'd never actually considered——

That was leaping ahead. What she had to do was decide something *now*—an unfair choice in itself, him or the work she was doing; the man she had loved and lived with, or a job in which she still wanted to prove herself.

Her thoughts jerked to a sudden halt. The man she *had* loved——'

Surely she still did, or she wouldn't be thrown into such confusion? And it was true, Daniel had made the first move, shown he really wanted her back, apologised . . . Some of the fault probably *had* been hers. Now she suddenly had the chance to put everything right. So why did she have to be pulled two ways, and muddled? Her mind seemed to swing wildly between old longings and a fierce, rebellious pride that told her he couldn't just beckon and expect her to come running. And then there was the question of an old love or a new, possibly utterly foolish, attraction . . .

An hour later she still hadn't got any further, and it was time to go down and present herself for lunch.

She went down in the slacks and blouse she had worn on the first day, hiding her morass of emotions behind a carefully calm face. Everything since she had come here was feeling suddenly unreal. She ran into Erik at the bottom of the stairs and received his beaming smile.

'I was thinking, Bet'anee, maybe you come running with me some time? We could make a good team at that too!'

'I suppose we have to fill in our time somehow!'

'Oh, it may change, we know we're a public relations exercise, but we still show them we can save lives, yes?' He was behind her as she walked into the sitting-room. 'I don't think we quit yet! You could be like Lang who pretends to be lazy but actually studies for his Fellowship while we have some free time!'

'Rats, Erik, are you knocking down my carefully cultivated playboy image?' Lang asked from an easy chair near the open window. His face showed something between amusement and defensiveness. 'Just because I asked you if I could borrow that book——'

'I don't see why you have to pretend, to study in secret! We're all ambitious, aren't we?'

Casual conversation was abruptly shattered by the sharp opening of a the far door. Neil was in the room in one movement and speaking as he came, with everyone else stilled into attention by his words.

'A call to the Mackenzie site's just come in. It's a blasting accident, with burns. Lang, it's you, me, and Peter. Where's Peter, upstairs?'

'No damn, he went down to the village to see why the Sunday papers didn't come! He should be back any minute——'

'Never mind. Lang, me and Bethany, then. Get ready!'

Bethany was moving even as he said her name. It didn't matter if he had chosen Peter first, her response was instant. The three of them moved rapidly towards the medical storage with Bethany's mind caught up in the quick calculations. Half of it was concentrating on what she would need, the other half listening to Neil.

'The paramedics'll do what they can, and they might be able to get some local help while we're on our way. We'll be six, seven hours getting there, minimum. Probability of internal injuries as well as the burns, I'd say: you've seen what blast force can do in the way of ruptures, Lang!'

'Sure have. What is it up there, mining?'

'Clearing for a new section of the gas pipeline. FTI got in on a consortium for it last year. Bethany, make sure you've got plasma packs as well as Pethilorfan and compounds, we're going to have shock to worry about almost the most . . .'

'Locals as well as drugs, yes? Petrol burns likely?'

'Could be, if there was a truck in the way of the blast. Allow for everything. No, don't rush it—five extra minutes this end might be worth its weight in gold the other!'

He could sound amazingly reassuring, and even smile at her with a comforting friendliness. It was like a total switch from his other, harder personality. Bethany was aware again, as she had been on the first day, of his capacity to do everything fast without appearing to hurry. When he paused to lift her flying jacket down from the peg for her she didn't take it as a criticism, since she had her hands full.

'Give me some of those and grab your thicker tracksuit from your locker, you can change into it in the plane. Hmm . . . There's one set of permanent equipment in there, so I don't think we need anything else from here. Lang, just take that for Bethany, will you? She's got the most to carry. I hear the chopper; we're off!'

Erik was there to watch them wistfully as they emerged from the house. Bethany guessed how much he wished he were coming with them, and gave him a sympathetic grin. He grinned back, sticking a large thumb in the air, and then turned to Neil with a look of calm.

'So anything else that comes in, Peter and I take it, yes?'

'Yes.' Neil hesitated briefly. 'If we find more injuries than they've told us, we may even send for you to come out in the second jet. I have to hope not, though. I'd rather have someone here. Over to you!'

It was a larger helicopter for the three of them, a matt-bodied one. They rose with the now familiar swaying motion. It seemed remarkably soon when the empty country between them began to change to scattered housing and straight roads instead of lanes twisting round hills; then there were the first outlying bunches of runway lights, and the low sprawl of warehouses and hangars around the flat edges of grass and tarmac. Their chopper pilot was murmuring laconically into his headset mike, confirming their emergency clearance. The answer he got sent him slanting leftwards away from the main part of the airport, and as Bethany looked down she saw a scattering of private planes. One of them was just beginning to creep out to take up position near the end of the runway.

The plane was marked with the international medical sign of the red cross on a white ground, and to show that it was theirs, below that was a version of the FTI logo—the triangle and initials, but with the Hippocratic staff and serpent added within it.

'Ah, our publicity sign,' Lang said drily. 'I wonder if each vice-president has a Lear jet with his name on? Or do they just peel things off and change them?'

Soon they were up the steps which had been pushed into place for them; the door was closing; someone who might be the co-pilot was pointing them towards seats and telling them to get belted in.

Bethany knew the drill after the Greenland trip with Erik, but it still made her brace her feet against the floor as they tore into the sky in a steep trajectory.

She glanced at the others and tried to imitate their easy relaxed manner. It was going to be a long trip before they even got there.

Over the next few hours she saw yet another facet of Neil. It was as if he could switch off the force of his personality at will to become quiet, amiable and unstressed, a practical team-leader but also a friendly colleague.

Not that he wasn't capable of being commanding too when he chose. Coffee and sandwiches were produced for them and, though both men tucked in with gusto, Bethany stopped after one sandwich. Then she found Neil leaning forward and planting the plate firmly in her lap.

'Eat. We missed lunch, and now we're travelling backwards along the clock—so you can take this as breakfast if you like, or last night's supper!'

'Thanks, but I often exist on coffee——All right,' she said quickly as she could see his amiable expression about to change into making it an order, 'and yes, you do have a point——'

'Right, so stoke up!'

For the energy they'd need later. Bethany didn't want to show that her appetite was gone because her mind was flying ahead. Burns had never been her favourite thing. She obediently started another sandwich—and then found that Neil had made some excuse to shift about, and that in doing so his hand came down briefly on her shoulder to give it a quick squeeze.

'Don't anticipate,' he said softly, his voice gentle where she would have expected it to be abrasive, 'we can all do that, but it doesn't help.' Then he was sitting back, and speaking at his normal level. 'Have you ever been up to north-west Canada, Lang? I can't remember.'

'No, I've only got as far as Newfoundland and that trip we did the first week to the injured geologist. I did have a girlfriend from Alberta once. What's it like up there—heavy timber and Injun country?'

'That's right. Spruce, poplar and jackpine. *Not* above the treeline this time,' Neil added, glancing at Bethany with a smile to include her in the conversation. 'The Mackenzie Valley lies between mountains and mountains, though we're going just to the south of that. It's an incredibly beautiful and wild part of the country. I suppose it's romantic of me to have a sneaking wish that civilisation would let it stay like that, and leave it alone!'

'I won't tell on you to our masters. Didn't I hear that the local Cree Indians or whoever wish they'd leave it alone too?'

'They managed to hold a large section of the project up for ten years on a land rights claim, yes. I don't blame them—but I think they've managed to sort it out with the government now.' Neil stretched and tipped back his seat in an easy motion. 'I've eaten, now I'm planning to catnap—but if anyone isn't going to do the same, wake me if a further radio report comes through!'

He closed his eyes, looking as relaxed as if he was on holiday. His lashes lay darkly above the lean cheekbones and his well-shaped hands were curled loosely against his thighs. Bethany glanced at him sidelong—and found herself wondering on a sudden memory whether it was his Inuit friend who had taught him how to ease down and withdraw into patience . . .

This morning seemed an incredibly long time ago, like something seen through the wrong end of a telescope. So did a certain telephone call she'd made afterwards——

She clamped down hard on that with an instant mental, *Not now!* But before the thought had quite vanished, she realised abruptly that she hadn't thought of Daniel once since the moment the emergency call came in. It was as if her mind had been wiped clean , like a slate.

CHAPTER EIGHT

'SWAB,' Neil said calmly, and the shrouded figure of the paramedic standing behind him carefully placed the forceps with their square of gauze into his outstretched hand.

The counter on the anaesthetic tanks hung steady. A generator hummed somewhere to break the concentrated quiet. Bethany kept the regular swell and depression of the patient's breathing carefully in one corner of her eye, sending a quick glance occasionally to the blood-pressure monitor attached to one flaccid arm, but from her seated angle watch with fascination as Neil's neat fingers worked steadily to repair a bad intestinal rupture.

At least they weren't faced with the primitive conditions she and Erik had been forced to. The prefabricated hut they were working in had been easy enough to turn into an operating theatre, clean and relatively sterile.

'How much of the whole blood we picked up at Yellowknife do we have left?' Neil asked without moving his eyes from his careful cut, swab, match and suture. The question was addressed generally, but it was Bethany who answered.

'Four. We left some of the plasma stocks for the burn patients, so we're beginning to run low on that too.'

'This laddie could really do with two more pints of whole blood, after what he's lost. Our next patient's still on his retaining drip, isn't he? We'll be through here soon and ready for him: Sandy, would you pass the word out?'

It was typical that Neil remembered the name of the volunteer who was standing by as dirty nurse. The beefy young man who, while not one of the paramedics, had been chosen to help because of his first aid training moved carefully to the door and remembered to shut it behind him before opening the second outer door. Bethany's mouth curved in an involuntary smile as she remembered that his only brief embarrassment had been at the necessity to dress up in a long robe and elasticated cap. Once dressed, he had done better at his task than some second-year nurses she had known.

They had left Lang at Yellowknife after a radio message which told them that the two severe burn cases had been airlifted out and taken there. There was a proper, if small, hospital at Yellowknife and for these two it had been their best option. The hospital passed the message that they'd be grateful for expert assistance just the same, so the team had split up.

Bethany and Neil had travelled on to the site where the other two casualties, both with internal injuries, had remained because they might rate a better chance if they weren't moved. As it was, they had both lost so much blood that there hadn't been a hope of trying repairs without massive blood transfusions as a first priority. Luckily each man's medical card had his blood group on it; luckily again, the hospital held an emergency stock and had it ready for them to pick up. Bethany had left them plasma and burn drugs in exchange.

If she had let herself, she could still be feeling stunned by the north Canadian scenery she had passed through, or flown across, in the past twenty-four hours. It was there in her memory, held like a series of photographs. The vastness of the Great Slave Lake, an unbelievable expanse of sheeny blue as they flew in over it; and as they wheeled to land, beyond the lake huge falls and rapids making brilliant white scratches against grey rock, grey-green scrub and forest. After she and Neil had taken off again from the busy small township of Yellowknife, changing this time to a light plane with a further two hundred miles still to go, there had been more of the same, as they flew across the lake again with distant glimpses of high mountains and miles of startingly vast wilderness. They made another rapid change to a helicopter, and the winding twists of the lower Mackenzie River came into view; a blue meander which vanished and reappeared amongst the dark blue-green of trees, with the yellow flash of sandbars islanding the blue water. It had seemed almost unreal to catch sight of the clear broad line of a main road, but that was the dramatic Mackenzie Highway carved out of the wild land to arrow northwards. They left it behind for forest again, protruding spikes of rock, a blue lake, a glimpse of falls seemingly frozen into cotton-wool . . . There was too much to take in, on too vast a scale, a huge area stretching to every horizon in wild beauty, so that Bethany had become dazed by the sheer expanse of it.

To arrive finally amongst humans in a cleared area with tidy roadways and huts and powerlines had seemed like being dumped in a positive metropolis . . .

'Right, I'm closing up,' Neil said, his voice laconic and steady. 'Blood pressure?'

'Holding. Pulse is—no it's OK. D'you want a count?'

'No, I'll leave it to you. Is Sandy back? Oh yes. Can you do a swab count for me? That's just telling me how many you've got there in the dishes. Thanks.' He listened as they were checked off, nodded absently, and then bent to his task again. He had shown remarkable patience with his semi-trained staff; patience altogether with an easy, friendly manner which drew Bethany's admiration. He had been quick and deft with the operation too, getting it done in the shortest possible time.

'I'm finishing off with clips, but a stitch round the drain. Right, all done. Give Dr Dale a minute and then we'll wheel him out.' He glanced towards Bethany and there was a quick gleam in his eyes—ruefulness, appreciation, a shared second professional communication. 'Guess we'd better clear up and then take a look at our next lad to see if he's ready . . .'

'I'm happy this end.' She was gently inserting an airway. The paramedic was directing his volunteer to stack the used instruments so that they could be removed. With no proper sterilisation facilities a new lot would be broken out for the next operation.

'Where did you train?' Neil asked the paramedic amiably.

'Vancouver for nursing. Then I went south to do the extra diploma the other side—over in Chicago. I didn't have the finance to train to be a doctor. Or the brains, probably,' he added with a shrug.

'Don't knock yourself, the work you're doing's first-rate. What the two of you managed before we got here deserves a medal.'

'Oh well . . .' The paramedic was trying not to look pleased.

'It's no more than the truth. Now; out with this one, gently does it—oh good, here's your work gang to transfer him to the medical hut. And some more to clean up our temporary theatre? Great organsation. Come on, Dr Dale—dump your present theatre gear to be burned, and we'll go and inspect our next!'

He had been calling her Dr Dale unremittingly ever since they got here. Bethany accepted it as a way to counter any doubts about her in this totally male world, but she slanted him a sidelong, half-mischevious smile as they emerged into the air. 'I'm ready when you are, Dr Jardine,' she said meekly—and saw his mouth move in a responsive smile of his own.

It was warm, something which had surprised her from the start in this far-north area; it was also, she had found out last night, plagued with clouds of

mosquitoes and blackfly. She absently scratched a
bite on her arm and waited for him to tell her not
to—which he promptly did, but with a friendly
ruefulness, rather than as a command.

'Don't do that or you'll remind of me of the one
in the middle of my back! At least they've managed
to keep the insects out of the theatre hut: I don't
much fancy operating under a mosquito net, do
you?' He grinned at her again as they walked
behind the patient, who was being transferred with
a careful steadiness by willing hands supporting his
stretcher. They both took a last look at him as the
stretcher party turned off to the hastily-cleared
recovery hut with their burden; then the two
doctors were moving away to the main medical
hut. As they went on Neil glanced down at
Bethany.

'You make a good partner. Do you want me to
say I'm just as glad you came as if it was Pete? I
might even stretch a point and say it's lucky he
went out!'

If she had been in a touchy mood she might have
given him a look to show she knew he wanted to
keep his operating team happy and therefore
smooth-running. She wasn't in a touchy mood.
She turned her head and smiled up at him. 'I'm
glad I came too, if you can believe that. Though,
I'll be even gladder when——Oh, what was *that*?'

The abrupt boom of a muffled explosion
somewhere at a distance made them both jump.
Bethany stiffened in sudden and immediate
apprehension, but her elbow was quickly caught in

Neil's grasp, though he let her go again at once. His voice spoke reassuringly, and with an exasperation which wasn't for her.

'They've begun blasting again. I'd forgotten they said they were going to start up again this afternoon. They've got a schedule to keep, I suppose!'

'I wonder how Lang's getting on . . .'

'As well as anyone could, and better than most. His record shows he's a dab hand with skin grafts.'

'Oh yes, they do grafts as a first dressing for heavy burns now, don't they?'

She had tried to make her voice casual, but Neil's arm brushed hers. It was an apparently accidental gesture, but it seemed to come in response to her tiny involuntary shiver. It was a relief to have been spared dealing with the severe burn cases, though she felt guilty for thinking so. She heard Neil's voice say with a quiet firmess, 'You'd have coped!'

'Oh, sure. I didn't——'

'You don't need to be defensive about it. We've all got something that gives us bad memories. What was it for you—a particularly nasty RTA where the cars went up in flames?'

'No, a house fire. Kids. Some idiot had left a half-full petrol tank lying around in a kitchen. It was when I was newly qualified. I don't really let it haunt me——'

'But it stays with you deep down. I know. We live with these things and carry on, all of us, don't we? Often, with more than a little help from our

friends.' Some memory was putting a wry note in
the deep tones, and a surprisingly uncritical
sharing. Their steps had brought them to the hut
where their second patient lay sedated and packed
with dressings, and Neil's voice snapped back into
practicality. 'Now, let's go and have a look at our
next laddie, and see if his blood pressure's come up
enough to let us operate!'

'I hope so, because he shouldn't really wait too
much longer.'

'I agree, so let's go and see.'

It wasn't until he answered her, amiably, that
Bethany remembered he was senior and the
decision lay with him. There had been no reproof
in his tone and it struck her how different he was
when working; generous instead of dominant, a co-
ordinator of skills instead of bossy . . . and with no
mean skills himself either, as she had been able to
see with unstinting approval. They had worked
together with an instant compatibility which could
sometimes happen, but was rare. Bethany's heart
gave a sudden squeeze and for a moment she was
almost distracted from her necessary
concentration. The feeling of unity it gave her to
work with Neil was striking, but this *wasn't* the
moment to feel as if a sudden dazzle of sunlight
had slipped into her bloodstream.

There was enough improvement to let the second
operation go ahead, and within a short time they
were back in the theatre hut. Someone had cleaned
it very thoroughly in their absence and there were
still wet slicks on the floor and the smell of

disinfectant in the air. The site's second paramedic was left in charge of the post-operative patient and the same team had reassembled in a fresh batch of emergency theatre clothes. This time there was also a new volunteer who had offered to be there as a message-taker and background non-sterile helper. Neil waited for Bethany to give the word, and then on her nod held out his hand to the paramedic.

'All right, Jim, scalpel, the one on the far left . . .'

Bethany watched his eyes narrow in concentration and felt a sudden certainty that everything would go well. It was in the best possible hands. For a few minutes she had little to do but watch Neil's deft movements, listen to the unflappable deep voice—and then disaster abruptly struck.

It wasn't a problem with the patient; Bethany had been monitoring his responses with care and they were blessedly steady. It wasn't even the new volunteer, it was Sandy who had worked so efficiently through the first operation. Perhaps it was over-confidence which made him step forward at the wrong moment—perhaps, in spite of the fact that he must be used to the noise, the sudden distant boom of another blast caught at his nerves because of recent memories—or perhaps his foot simply slipped on the wet floor. Neil's certainly did, as he twisted sharply away to avoid the unsterile touch. Before Bethany could do more than gasp he had staggered off balance and fallen, to land with a bruising thud on the floor.

'Don't help me up!' It was immediate, before the

horrified Sandy could even bend. 'Patient, Bethany?'

He hadn't jolted the table. 'OK, no change,' she responded crisply. 'You'll need fresh gloves, yes——?'

It was worse than that, she saw at once as he came to his feet. The instrument he had been holding had flown across the room with a clatter, but he was wincing and his thumb was bent sideways at a peculiar angle. His *right* thumb, on his operating hand . . .

'It's—out, I think,' he said in a breathless voice which was obviously tight with pain.

Jim, the paramedic, let out an exclamation. The others were frozen in horror, particularly Sandy. Then Neil's voice came again with a forced calm.

'I'll have a sterile towel to wrap round this, and *one* fresh glove. Then Dr Dale and I will change places. Luckily she happens to be a highly experienced surgeon as well as her other talents. Bethany, you come down here and take over, and give me a quick run-down on anything I should particularly watch for.'

The steadiness of his voice minimised everyone's panic and Bethany was geared into action before he had finished speaking. 'Fine,' she said briskly, copying his calm, 'yes, I can see what you're doing. I'll keep an eye on both ends while you get settled and then we'll carry on!'

There was Sandy to calm first, a valuable few minutes lost in his stammering guilt. There was a carefully hidden panic of her own in case she wouldn't cope, had forgotten too much—but it left her the minute they re-started, and her hands seemed to know what to do while her brain was still groping. She and Neil worked with a verbalised co-ordination. From him, there was, 'You can see where I put the first clamp, and I was just about to cut down beyond that,' and then later, 'Watch that small intestine, I'm not sure if there's a tear or if it's just massive bruising . . .' From her, 'Keep your eye on the dial for a moment and tell me if it starts to swing,' and, 'There's dopomine there if the blood pressure goes into a noticeable drop . . .' It was somehow so easy to anticipate each other that it was almost like one identity with two bodies, but with the reassurance of each other's added skills.

Bethany had almost forgotten what it was like to walk the knife-edge between too fast for caution, and too slow for a dangerously ill patient. When she finally closed up she could feel the sweat beading her forehead and making little runnels down the back of her neck. Her eyes, and her mind, told her that she had done everything that could be done. And there had been no sudden alarms. Brown eyes above her mask sought for blue ones and found a light of approval glowing in them.

'Good. I'll have to get you to come back and check here, I'm too hamfisted for the airway——'

'*And* too injured.' In spite of the light in his eyes Bethany could see the tightness of pain in the muscles of his neck. 'Jim, if you can get your people to move the patient *very* gently out—and keep your eyes on the drip as you go, he'll need a replacement within about ten minutes, I'd say—I'll have a look at Neil's—Dr Jardine's hand.'

'I'll see to everything and come back. Um—I don't know if it's one of your skills, Doctor, but I'm trained in manipulation, so if it's just a dislocation . . .'

He had spoken to Bethany, with respect, but it was Neil who answered before she could. 'Good man. It doesn't feel like a break, just bloody uncomfortable! Sandy——' In spite of everything Neil could give time to the unwitting culprit. Time and reassurance. 'You weren't to blame, it was my own clumsiness,' he said firmly and with deliberate sincerity. 'No, I mean it! And congratulations on sticking with it in spite of the panics, you did really well. If you ever decide to do paramedic training like Jim, I'll give you a reference any day. You *all* did well, and thanks!'

They were suddenly alone in the theatre hut. Bethany should probably have gone with the others to keep a check on her patient, as she might have done wearing her anaesthetist's hat; but she had developed a healthy respect for Jim's capabilities. 'Let me see,' she demanded.

'I . . . think we'll let Jim see; it doesn't look like a break.' Neil unwrapped the sterile towel from his right hand all the same and held it away from him with a wince. 'Of all the things to happen——'

'It's going to swell nastily, even if he can put it back. Has it ever happened before?'

'I don't usually fall over in operating theatres!' he caught himself up on the inclination to snarl,

and his mouth moved in a painful smile which
abruptly and without warning tore at her heart.
'No, it isn't a loose joint that slips out from time to
time. And yes, my dear girl, it hurts; worse than a
nagging tooth, if you want to know! I don't dare
try to jerk it back with my other hand . . .*Do* you
count manipulation amongst your professional
skills?'

'No, and I won't try it, if we've got someone
here who's an expert. It was nice of you to say it
wasn't his fault—the young one, I mean.'

'He couldn't help it. I'd like to scrag the
foreman who gave the order to restart blasting.
There must be several of the crew who haven't
forgotten what happened last time.' Neil winced as
Bethany's gentle fingers probed his palm; then,
abruptly, his other hand had closed over hers to
hold it tightly. 'You thoroughly earned your keep
today, didn't you. You were damn good, and we'd
have lost him without you. You're really quite a
lady behind that delicate and far too attractive
appearance, Dr Dale . . .'

A sudden and unexpected shyness made Bethany
want to pass it off with a light comment, if only she
could have thought of one. Instead she found
herself looking down into that familiar lean face
without a word to say; only with her heart
beginning an unwary, uneven beat, and her mouth
softening into a responsive smile. They seemed to
gaze at each other for a long moment, time
stretching, every nerve bewitched as Neil looked up
at her from his seated position and she looked

down at him . . . and then he turned his head away sharply as the door opened with the return of Jim.

The next few moments were obviously painful for Neil and brought forth, without apology, a muttered but savage expletive. The treatment was obviously effective, however, and with his thumb back in its proper place he agreed to go in search of a cold compress—once he had checked on his patients. Bethany told him firmly that *she* would do that, and left him. She felt uncommonly light of heart. There were good reasons for it: both their patients were doing well, and she could feel proud with the way she had snapped back into being a surgeon for the second case. Word seemed to have gone round among the site workers too, and she was greeted with an exceptionally respectful. 'Hi, Doc!' by several of the men she passed. .

None of it, somehow, provided an adequate reason for the euphoria that gilded the trunks of the surrounding pines, made the sky above an extra dazzling blue, lent the practical tidy lines of huts an air of charm their practicality actually lacked . . .

She didn't see Neil again for an hour. She was beginning to wonder where he might have got to when she caught sight of him walking towards her with his arm in a sling and a tightly thoughtful look on his face which a few days ago she might have thought didn't bode well. She had just emerged from checking their two post-operative patients again and she waited for him to come up to her, then gave him a look which fell halfway between sympathy and sunniness.

'I've just done a post-op round, and both our men are holding their own nicely. In fact, improving very satisfactorily. I had a look at the minor burn cases too, though they were all well enough not to need any interference from me. So, how's the hand?'

'Not comfortable, and I could have done without being force-fed on strong painkillers and told I ought to lie down for half an hour. I don't really need this, either, but I had to let them put it on! All right, don't tell me I'm ungrateful, I know. Ah—' Neil was regarding her and an intrigued, humorous expression had crept into his eyes—'you haven't turned into Dracula, by any chance, have you?'

'*What*?'

'A pink tinge round the mouth . . .'

Bethany put her hand guiltily to her lips, then chuckled. 'Oh, help, does it show? Someone gave me some wild rasberrries, apparently they grow here in great bunches when it's summer! And very nice too!'

'We'll need to fly our patients out as soon as they're out of shock. That ought to be as soon as we can.' From looking as if he wanted to laugh, Neil had drawn in all at once into officialdom. Bethany rapidly tried to pull herself together into the same attitude. 'What's your opinion, Dr Dale, do you think we might be able to get them moved within the next day?'

'I'd say so. You want to get back to

Yellowknife?'

'I think we should—for the patients and for us.'

'Yes, of course.' Lang might be needing help. It was a thought to put an involuntary damper on her mood and then to make her scold herself for that directly afterwards; but Neil's next words denied her supposition.

'I've just been on the radio. Lang feels he's got plenty of assistance there, but he's going to need some extra time because he wants to do a second session after his first. Once we've hospitalised our patients we'll be at a loose end. So I was thinking . . .'

'Yes?'

'*I'm* no use to anyone like this, and Erik and Peter are apparently not over-occupied at Achnabrae. In the circumstances it would seem like a waste of the company's money to rush two of us back rather than waiting. So I'm thinking of seeing if I can hitch a lift on a supply plane up to Marker Lake for a couple of days. Would you like to come with me?'

'I'd—I'd love to . . . Marker Lake, did you say? Where's that?'

'It's up in what's called the Barren Grounds. It's tundra, and in winter it's under snow, but at this time of year it comes to life. There's just a tiny settlement, and a place on the edge of that is where I used to work. Good, then; if everything goes on progressing well here, I'll try and arrange it!'

Neil turned and walked away. Bethany was left with her pulse suddenly going into an uneven race.

The words had been casual, even formal—but she was sure she had caught a certain glimmer of meaning behind the thoughtfulness in his eyes . . .

He might just have wanted to show her where he used to work. He might just——But it was a definite suggestion that they should go off together for a couple of days, away from FTI, away from the need to stick to a carefully professional relationship. Back home, there would have been no doubt of what he meant by that.

The distant boom of another blasting explosion seemed no louder than the sudden thump of her heart. A dazzle seemed to run through her blood again with a race of excitement, as she acknowledged that she didn't care *what* he meant.

In the last hours, something seemed to have been silently acknowledged between them; something on both sides, inevitable, unspoken, but very real.

CHAPTER NINE

THEY FLEW to Marker Lane in a small plane packed with crates. The pilot seemed perfectly happy to have them along and obviously viewed the five-hundred-mile flight in the same light as a quick hitch along the motorway. He chatted amiably above the steady drone of the engine, in the Canadian accent Bethany had grown used to over the last few days.

The fact that Neil had worked up here provided an instant point of reference. The huge spread of distance that covered this area seemed no bar to their having accquaintances in common. It was like listening to two people exchanging small-town news as she heard, 'Yeah, they had a lot of trouble with drunks at the Skating Festival again this spring, ended up with a lock-up full of Indians,' and, 'No, Sam's not still around, his old lady persuaded him to quit and go back to Ontario. She never quite settled.'

Bethany kept quiet in the background, but gave a quick smile as she was offered a casual, friendly, 'You all right on that crate, Bethany? Sorry not to be able to offer you a proper seat, we use the space!'

'I'm fine, thanks. It's nice of you to take us!'

'No problem. You might as well see as much of the country as you can if it's your first trip. Mind you, not many people choose the Barrens to visit, it's some of the emptiest country alive. It kind of gets to you, though. All you can see down below you now'd be a white wasteland in winter: I almost prefer it then, funnily enough.'

He had already shown that he knew all about the pipeline-accident and the casualties they'd come to treat, discussing them with a sympathetic interest. In spite of the vastness of this land, everyone seemed to know everything about everybody. It was difficult not to feel a shaft of self-consciousness on that thought to bring colour up into her cheeks . . .

She looked hastily out of the nearest porthole to distract herself, resisting the temptation to cast a glance under her lashes at Neil. The view below was fascinating enough, anyway. It was like an infinite watery jigsaw puzzle. Half the land seemed to be covered by lakes. Rivers broad and narrow wound like gleaming snakes amongst green and brown land stretching in an incredible emptiness to every horizon, a glistening lacework of water and land. Stands of trees were scattered like dots; here there was the sudden vivid greenness of a valley, there a flat expense of silvery-brown against the sharper cut of a river channel. It looked as primeval as if no living thing had ever existed down there, but there was a strange, eerie beauty about its endless flatness and desolation.

'Have you spotted any caribou?' Neil's voice asked from close beside her, and he leaned across with his shoulder brushing hers companionably. 'There should be some, this time of year. Musk ox too, though they're probably all up in the game sanctuary.'

'You mean something does actually *live* there?'

'A lot of things. The musk ox are there all year round, so are the arctic foxes and wolves. And the grizzlies, but they hibernate in winter. Then there are the lemmings——'

'Flinging themselves off cliffs?'

'Not round here, they seem to be too busy being preyed on to be suicidal. The caribou don't come down until the spring . . . There used to be Inuit living here too, though that's harder to believe. They moved away when the caribou herds declined.' Neil paused, and the warmth of his shoulder against her seemed to send a distracting languor through her. 'I'm trying to see if I can spot any snow geese for you. It's not the right time to see them flying in huge migrating flocks, and they'll be hard to see against the sun if they're only in two's and threes. It's actually quite a hive of industry down there in the summer, whatever it looks like from up here!'

'It just looks—as if it goes on for ever!'

'Not quite. It's all permafrost underneath, though—iron-hard, with only the top surface melting and allowing things to grow. That's why you get the wild-life—their last refuge before the High Arctic. Those are tundra lakes down there, and tundra meadows, and if you were down there amongst them you'd be able to see sedge and grass and flowers—all sorts of flowers, blooming away like crazy for their short life span before the ice and snows come back.'

'You make it sound like a short life but a merry one,' Bethany said—and then wished that his nearness, and the way his breath brushed her cheek, hadn't distracted her into sounding flippant.

'I was thinking more about revival. The way the winter looks as if it's killed everything, but then you find it hasn't—that after the long dark, life's still there after all.' Neil's words seemed to hang thoughtfully in the air. Then he sat back abruptly, had moved away from her, and was raising his voice to call out to the pilot. 'What are you carrying on this trip, Joe—foodstuffs, or hardware?'

'Mostly hardware, but there's a load of flour somebody wanted. Tell you what else I've got—oranges! Some government department seems to have issued a directive about vitamin C, so there was a crate of them to go.'

'With instructons in two languages to say they're for eating, not for decoration? I wouldn't put anything past them!'

Neil's words brought forth an appreciative chuckle as if they both knew what he was talking about, and led on to a conversation of which Bethany only caught snatches. She was caught between wishing Neil hadn't moved away from her, and a relief that he had because every muscle had suddenly ached to lean against him, to curl into the grasp of his uninjured arm like a homecoming. And here, now, wasn't the right time.

She didn't know what had happened to her in the past few days, but there was such a sureness inside her of attraction returned, of questions silently asked and answered, that it was like an electric current running between them. Neil's seeming casualness might have made her feel uncertain if it weren't for that, but she was as sure of what it masked as she was of her own tingling awareness. It was heady, joyful, the culmination of something which seemed to have started the moment they met across a formal interview in a Glasgow hotel; and it seemed only to grow under the care of concealment.

Perhaps, she thought fancifully, with a smile curving her mouth, it was even what he had meant to convey in the sudden seriousness of his voice—that things grew secretly in the dark as they did in the lands below, then burst into daylight suddenly in full bloom.

He was back to touch her on the arm as they came in to land, pointing down at what seemed to be the merest scattering of houses clustering round a long river inlet. There were small figures to be seen moving to and fro, one or two faces turned upwards, an arm here and there raised in a cheerful wave. The houses were low and flat, obviously prefabricated again, a universal whitish grey but with a sudden bright colour showing on a door here and there; and someone had raised a short metallic steeple as a gesture on what must be a church. Then they were coming in to make a slightly bumpy landing on a cleared space away from the river.

'You'll find it's colder here, summer or no summer . . .' With the words Neil reached a hand round Bethany's back to pull up her hood, the touch and his smile feeling like a caress. 'Come on, let's get out, and go and surprise a few people!'

Joe was going on north from here when he had

unloaded part of his cargo and refuelled. It had already been arranged that he would pick them up again in two days to fly them back to Yellowknife on his return journey. It didn't seem to matter what time; they'd know when he arrived. As Bethany emerged from the plane she found that Neil was lifting her down in a strong, easy grip in spite of his swollen thumb, from which he had long ago discarded the sling. She landed unsteadily on spongy, mossy ground in which her eye was immediately caught by tiny crushed flowers.

She didn't have time to look at them. Neil was guiding her onwards, and almost at once he was being greeted by welcoming voices.

One or two of them spoke in English, but more were in a sharp guttural language full of clicking consonants. One of two of the smiling faces which suddenly surrounded them were European, though with a lean, weathered look—but most were round and flattened with vividly dark eyes, a thickly opaque pale skin, shiny tufts of straight black hair . . . They were like pictures out of a childhood book on the Eskimo.

Everyone seemed to want to buffet Neil on the shoulder and he was answering greetings in the same clicking language. Bethany received her share of smiles too, with flashing curious glances from slanting black eyes.

Neil must have said something to let them escape from the crowd, because within moments he had pulled Bethany to move on again, calling something over his shoulder. His face was alight with laughter and he was smiling still as he looked down at her. 'You look a bit dazed. Sorry about that!'

'What on earth were you saying? I couldn't understand a word!'

'My Inupiaq's along way from perfect, but they tolerate my mistakes because I try. I was telling everyone not to let on I'm here—and I'm going to drag you on a quick walk now, because I want to get to the clinic house before the word *has* gone ahead! It's not far—the last building on the edge of the settlement, but that's no distance!'

Bethany's legs were a little stiff from sitting in the plane and she would have liked time to look around and take everything in, but his rapid stride was carrying them onwards with such cheerful enthusiasm that she hurried to keep up with him. His obvious joy gave her a lift of the heart; so did the equally obvious pleasure with which he had been greeted. They came quickly through the small wide-spaced and reached a long low building with open land beyond it—a greening land scattered with sudden bursts of tall golden poppies and silvery, silky-topped grasses to make Bethany let out a gasp of surprised delight. Then, just as they came up to this last and larger building with its windows glinting in the bright sunlight, a door opened and the portly form of a male Eskimo emerged.

He looked at Neil with his jaw dropping, and then broke into an immediate glad welcome.

'Neil! It can't be——Oh, but this is excellent——'

'Hallo, John! We were passing this way, so to speak—well, near enough to make it impossible not to come up, anyway! How are you, and how's everything?'

'Well enough. We have a new children's room built on to the back now, thanks to the money you've been sending! You came in on the supply plane? Does——'

'I hope not, I'm aiming for surprise. Oh, Bethany, this is Dr John Takavluk, the very able medical man who tends the settlement's ills—and acts as the clinic's sole medicine man too since my desertion. John, this is Bethany Dale, who works with me as a surgeon-anaesthetist.'

'I'm delighted to meet you,' John said courteously, holding out a hand. 'Surgeon-anaesthetist, eh? I have to do a bit of that myself from time to time. I suppose you wouldn't care for a job?'

'I'm not letting you poach her, she's far too useful!'

'As she also would be to the Inuit people here. You see, I have no conscience about recruiting!' John's look of amusement denied that he was seriously urging Bethany to take up a job here, and she met a friendly gaze from the alert dark eyes as they exchanged a handshake. His was firm and definite. 'You are very welcome,' he said with a touch of formality. 'May you often return! Neil——'

He broke off, a smile suddenly lighting his black eyes as someone came round the far corner of the building with a child on either hand. Bethany had the glimpse of a trousered but distinctly feminine form, short, shining, russet hair, a solemn loveliness in a downturned face. Then Neil had put two fingers in his mouth, and a raucous whistle abruptly split the air.

The girl's head jerked upwards in disbelief. Then she had let the children go and was running like a deer towards the group by the door, all flying long legs on booted feet. Neil stepped forward to catch her, his cheek going against hers as he gave her an encompassing hug.

They were almost of a height, and as the girl drew back without letting him go entirely, Bethany saw a radiant happiness in the wide grey eyes looking into his face.

'Neil! Oh why didn't you *tell* us you were coming . . .'

'I didn't know until the last minute. Cathy, love—' he turned her round so that she was facing Bethany, though he still hadn't let her go, 'Look, I've brought someone with me—she's a colleague, and I wanted her to meet you. Bethany Dale, Catherine Anderson. Catherine,' he said to Bethany, 'is a nursing Sister. And she runs this place.'

A cold lump seemed to have lodged in the middle of Bethany's chest. It had something to do with the pride in his face as he presented the tall, beautiful girl who stood in the circle of his arm; more than something to do with their obvious familiarity, the taken-for-granted unity with which they stood together. Catherine Anderson *was* beautiful too, truly lovely, with one of those faces painters would always long to paint, photographers to photograph. Winged eyebrows matched the dark russet of her hair and its very short shining cut did nothing to detract from the perfect curve of her cheek, the elegant straightness of nose and chin.

Her smile was lovely too, as she offered it to Bethany with a genuineness which was reflected in the grey eyes, and stepped forward to clasp her hand.

'What a brilliant surprise! Hallo, Bethany, I'm so glad Neil's brought you!'

Her voice had a soft Canadian accent that warmed the simple words. Sheer niceness shone out of her—and, Bethany thought as something inside her seemed abruptly to wither, she also held that glow, the simple confidence of knowing she was loved—obviously, by the man who still stood beside her and looked at her with so much affection that it was painful to watch.

Bethany hid her numbness behind a smile. She took care not to avoid Neil's eyes while she kept her own very carefully friendly. She said how glad she was to be here. Then the Inuit doctor went away and the other three of them went indoors.

They were to stay here, it seemed. Rooms were rapidly found for them. It was a single room each—though Bethany couldn't help a supposition that Neil's might not be slept in. That wasn't her business, not now—but oh, it was ironic that she had let her own awakening feelings draw her into quite different expectations when, as it turned out, all Neil had evidently wanted to do was introduce her to his steady, long-term girlfriend . . .

She wondered why Neil had ever left here, when there was this lovely girl he plainly loved, and who plainly loved him.

It was in a pause for relaxation after Catherine had shown her proudly round the Inuit clinic—half medical facility, half home for the displaced homeless—that she found out.

They were sitting on a wooden balcony running along the back of the building. Catherine called it 'the stoop' and it was obviously a summer sitting-room, in spite of a sharpness in the air under the bright warmth of the sun. Coffee—or something answering to that name—had been offered in thick mugs, but Neil had taken his to inspect the new addition to the building which jutted out into an L-shape on one corner. Catherine's eyes had followed him affectionately until he was out of sight; but then she spoke thoughtfully.

'I guess I was right to boot him out back into the world. It was time!'

'Oh?'

'When he came here it was after Sarah, his wife, died, and he needed time and space and something to get his head back together. He'd worked himself into the ground trying to forget, and trying to stop blaming himself——'

'Blaming himself? Why?' The question was jerked out of Bethany involuntarily. It was something to learn suddenly that Neil had ever had a wife. 'Sorry,' she mumbled rapidly, 'I—it's not my business, I shouldn't ask!'

'It's OK. It's a long time ago now. She died of an unexpected subdural haemorrhage. Neil was away, the other end of the country at some conference or other. Being a neuro-surgeon himself, of course he felt that if he'd been there . . . Who's to say that he could have done anything anyway? But it made it worse that she was expecting their first child.'

'Oh no!'

'Fraid so. Anyway . . . That was five years ago, and he went on working for a year, maybe eighteen months, knocking himself out in the same place, same job, all the memories—Hardly surprising that in the end he just walked out one day. He said then that he was finished with surgery altogether. I suppose he was having a nervous breakdown, if you like to look at it that way. Anyway, he ended up here; far away as he could get, I guess. Then after a while he started work—we were short of a doctor, particularly one who'd work for nothing, and could deal with anything surgical that came up besides! As to that,' Catherine added with her lovely smile touched with ruefulness, 'we still are, though John's here now and does what he can!'

'You said you . . . booted Neil out?'

'I told him to go off and earn some money for us,' Catherine said. 'Not that we didn't need it—we do, so that made it a real excuse—but I thought *he* needed it too. The impetus. He'd been here all of two years and there was a lot of talent he was wasting. I knew if he didn't go back . . . Well, he *has* gone back, and I can see he's got all his old interest back! Pity about the job, but even the money he's been able to send so far has got us so many extras! The new building, for one, we couldn't have done that without him!'

Bethany was absorbed in the facts she was taking

in. So *that* was what Neil was doing at Achnabrae—supporting an Inuit clinic a thousand miles across the world. She could feel an involuntary question swelling within her, and had to ask it.

'What was she like—his wife? Or—sorry, perhaps you didn't know her!'

Catherine gave a little sigh and the chair she was sitting in creaked briefly, but when Bethany glanced across at her in apology she was smiling. 'It's funny to hear someone ask if I knew her. Yes . . . She was my cousin, and we grew up together. We're the same age, so everyone used to take us for twins, as a matter of fact!'

'Oh! I—I'm even more sorry then, I shouldn't have asked——'

'Don't worry. I don't know why you should have known, if Neil didn't say.' It didn't seem to occur to her that he might not have said anything at all—about Catherine herself. 'We weren't really so alike, just a family resemblance,' the soft voice said easily. 'And then we did the same things to a certain extent. We went through nursing training together at the same hospital. Then I went to Montreal as I'd always planned, and after a while I was sent here. Sarah had gone to England and met Neil and they were married. It was just a year later when she died. She was only twenty-five. Do you know, it's only when I think of her that I remember I'm thirty?'

She sounded so surprised that Bethany almost joined her in her silvery laughter. She supposed Catherine could be thirty, though she had the kind of face that looked ageless. There was silence for a moment and then Catherine's voice came again with a brighter note in it. 'It's really good to see that he's picked up on life again! He was too much of an idealist in the old days, that always makes everything harder. But, as I said, pity about the job; though I suppose it *has* at least put him back into the swim again!'

'Why a pity? Oh—because of all the rules and regulations—?' It was suddenly so obvious that Bethany felt foolish for having asked. Catherine might originally have been Neil's cousin-in-law, but she was something more now. And the FTI job, with its refusal to accept the distraction of fiancées, was probably their one bar to an openness about their future. Catherine's voice broke in.

'No, I meant a pity about the way it's turned out. Neil's last letter said it wasn't working out the way any of you expected. In fact, he was beginning to think there was something heavy involved financially. Like the company wanting to make a big tax loss, so they set up something that cost a lot and looked philanthropic. And then they'll simply ditch it.' A tiny frown had drawn Catherine's brows together as she looked at Bethany's startled face. 'Oh dear, shouldn't I have passed that on? I thought——'

'If we're just a tax loss we'll be a huge one! The equipment alone——'

'Mm, Neil said that too, but he also said big companies are pretty cynical, and that most of the time you're so under-used that the whole thing doesn't make much sense. Oh well—disappointing, but your time hasn't *all* been wasted, has it? Even if he's right, and your contracts do get cancelled before time! Anyway,' Catherine said, giving Bethany a suddenly cheerful look, 'in some ways that will be no bad thing, will it?'

The conversation ended there abruptly with someone calling her from the house, but she had given Bethany plenty to think about. There seemed to be no end to the shocks which were going to bombard her, or to a cold and reasonable truth bent on forcing her to live in the real world. It was a bitter irony that her heart could turn over still with her new knowledge about Neil's past—when he had had the lovely, likeable Catherine to comfort him. Ironic too that, Catherine notwithstanding, Bethany could feel an ache of wistfulness at the thought of leaving Achnabrae because it meant leaving him.

She could only jeer at herself and go on behaving as if these two long days were exactly as she had expected. They *were* long days too: at eleven-thirty p.m. the light was only just fading into dusk and at two the sun rose again. Bethany tried to occupy herself by helping Catherine with the Inuit children who flocked around the clinic, and with the old people who greeted her with a shy courtesy. She let Neil take her inland a little way to admire the flowers and the birds—including larks which sang with a sweetness to break the heart in this strange burgeoning land, and the more sinister flocks of black ravens, and the taloned white gyrfalcons. She took care that some of the children came with them, which wasn't hard because their brightness and their clicking language fascinated her, and she could truthfully say so.

She could also truthfully claim to be tired. It gave her an excuse to withdraw to her room early and leave Catherine some time alone with Neil. Even so she could hear their murmuring voices out on the stoop, their tones bespeaking a gentle intimacy. After that first hug, they seemed to be careful not to show affection to each other in public—but it was there, in the easy way they treated each other . . .

She had shut herself into her room early on the second and last night of their stay, but she was still thoroughly awake when a tap came on her door. 'Bethany?' Catherine's voice asked. 'There's something that's worth waking up for, do come out, I don't want you to miss it!'

'Yes? What——?

'It's just dark enough for you to see the Aurora Borealis. Come on!'

Bethany's hand was seized to pull her outside. 'Go on, look up,' Catherine urged with an obvious pleasure, 'no, come over here away from the house, you'll see it better . . .'

The extraordinary brilliance in the sky seemed to flash and whirl, a canopy of dancing green-white ghosts. Bethany was caught by enchantment. 'Oh, it's incredible, and just like *fireworks!'*

'It's merely a natural phenomenon,' Neil's voice said in the dusk behind her, which made Catherine turn on him.

'Oh, you, stop trying to sound like Nanuk's grandfather! You know how fascinated *you* were when you first came out—you used to come outside and stare for hours!'

'I plead guilty. And I'm happy to share it with Bethany. I *was* wondering if it was such a highly concentrated fish diet which was making her so quiet——'

'It's understandable for her to be worn out after flying about and operating and then flying about again! You should treat her more gently, Neil, not everyone lives on bursts of energy like you! Now, having woken her up—' Catherine touched Bethany's arm with gentle apology—'I'm going to bed myself. So goodnight, children!'

Bethany would have gone herself if Neil hadn't been standing in her way. She satisfied herself by looking up at the stars again. Their incredible brilliance dazzled and danced across the sky. She tried not to be aware of the shadow beside her which was Neil, until he said,

'Glad you came?'

'Yes, of course. I like Catherine tremendously!'

'She likes you too. I thought you might get on. You *have* seemed—well, quiet since we got here, though. Are you all right?'

'I think I'm suffering from reaction. Maybe culture shock too,' Bethany added with a deliberately contrived laugh, 'it's a—an incredible difference, coming this far north! And I keep wondering how they manage when they can't grow crops or anything——'

'They eat seal and narwhal, caribou if they can get it, blubber for extra vitamins—it's an incredibly high-protein diet. One problem, of course, is that when the Inuit give up their proper hunting there's nothing

else for them but government or charitable handouts.
Quite apart from wiping a lot of them out with
measles in the early days—'

'Did we? Not on purpose!'

'No, of course not, just giving them a bug they'd
never met. I was saying, quite apart from that, the
opening up of the Arctic for geological surveys and
oil explorations has taken away the region's original
culture—without putting anything real, for them, in
its place. Are we really going to stand out here discussing the Inuit?'

'Not if you don't want to. How long has Catherine
worked out here?'

'Cathy? Four years. That's a longer spell than
most, and she's due to go back soon. Oh—you know
that carving from a bit of narwhal's tusk that you
admired? She wants to give it to you, as a memento.'

'She can't—it's beautiful! I didn't mean her
to——'

'She has a rule against holding on to possessions.
Mind you, I'm not sure if she'll ever bring herself to
part with her sealskin boots!' There was a laugh in
Neil's voice. Then it sobered to a deep note and he
began, 'Bethany——'

His hand had touched her shoulder and he must
have felt her flinch away. He withdrew at once—and
for Bethany, with a deep confused ache inside her, it
was as if even the brightness in the sky above dimmed
just a little. 'You're tired, and Joe will be back to
fetch us tomorrow,' he said. 'Goodnight, go back to
sleep!'

It was outrageous to feel the magnetism still, and

wish he had gone on touching her. It was outrageous to imagine that he had wanted to—when she must have been wrong about that from the start. Unless he was the same sort of philanderer as Daniel, taking what offered. And surely he wouldn't dare, out here in the half-light of the far north, with his real love only yards away in the house . . .

He stepped back to let her pass, and she took her bitter thoughts to bed with her.

CHAPTER TEN

THEY HAD been back at Achnabrae a week and Neil was in a bad temper.

He seemed to have been in a permanently ill-natured mood ever since they got back. Bethany could make several guesses as to the underlying reasons. First there was the lack of work: Erik and Peter hadn't had anything to do while the rest of the team were gone and even the rigs seemed to be maintaining a continual state of good health. Then there was a call to the southern end of Greenland, and Neil obviously wanted to go himself but felt obliged to let Erik and Peter go—particularly since his own thumb was still marginally sore—and to cap it all they came straight back to say they'd arrived to find their patient had already been hospitalised and satisfactorily dealt with.

'And I suppose they just *forgot* to send a cancelling message?' Neil snarled.

'It looks like it. What do you want us to do now—make a casualty round to the nearer rigs?'

'No, they're all on a "nothing to report", so going round might look like treading on their nursing staff's toes. I suggest you put your feet up and practise being useless!'

Neil's stinging tone in answer to Peter's polite question made Lang look round with raised eyebrows

—though he left it until Neil had gone out of the room. '*What* has got into our beloved leader?' he enquired of the air.

'I think maybe he's a frustrated workaholic,' Erik said, with a grin at Bethany, 'and when your trip to Canada's over he's like an addict without his fix. What do you think, Bet'anee?'

'Something like that. It's frustrating for all of us.'

For Neil there was a very good reason for discontent too—leaving his Catherine behind at a far distance, when with acres of empty time here, he might as well have stayed. Leaving his Catherine anyway . . . No wonder he had been in a silent and withdrawn mood all the way back to Yellowknife, only coming out of it to chat with a forced cheerfulness to Joe as he piloted them back. And now, back at Achnabrae, he was downright bad-tempered.

'I guess maybe I wait for him to be in a good mood before I ask him if I can go down to Glasgow to fetch some things my uncle's left for me there,' Erik commented. 'Would you say so, Bet'anee?'

'Don't ask my opinion. I think he'll be bloody-minded if he doesn't let you go, though—there's plenty of us here!'

She ought to go down to Glasgow herself. It was what she had meant to do—wasn't it?—before the Canada trip. The trouble was that it seemed a dim memory now, as if her sudden agonising over Daniel had been the last kick of an old attraction which had actually died. And been replaced——

Replaced much too easily, when it was something she had believed in. Perhaps she shouldn't blame

Daniel so much for his capacity to *flit*—when she had only had to be thrown into contact with a dynamically attractive man to find herself blown apart with longings, chasing rainbows, dreaming dreams . . . She ought to telephone Daniel and give him an answer, even if it was no, at least that. And it did seem as if it was going to be no; because even now, in spite of everything, she felt a churning inside whenever Neil came anywhere near her!

The carving Catherine had pressed on her acted as a salutary reminder. She kept it on a shelf in full view, deliberately.

It was a beautiful little thing, a small piece of narwhal tusk delicately carved into a pair of baby seals tumbling together. They looked so lifelike that they almost seemed to move, yet they were stylised too. It had been carved by an old man, a former great hunter amongst the Inuit but now just one of the crowd who lived on government relief. Apparently he stubbornly refused to use his carving talent commercially; to him it was simply a skill he used for his own enjoyment, and he still saw himself as a hunter, not as some kind of *merchant*. Bethany hadn't wanted to take something so treasurable which had obviously been given to Catherine as a gift, but the other girl had insisted . . .

Bethany knew she ought to be making decisions rather than letting herself drift. If Neil's theory was right, this job wouldn't last for ever anyway. All the same, she couldn't bring herself to do anything except exist behind the polite appearance of normality, chatting to the others, reading, sharing mealtimes, watching television programmes. She even let Erik persuade her into exercising in the gym again, in his company, though his unremitting energy was wearing.

'I think I've had enough. I'm going to sit outside in the sun and get *brown*. If we're going to have a good summer for once, and I'm not shut up in a hospital missing it for once, I don't see why I should waste it! And no, thanks, I don't want to go for a run, I'm feeling stretched enough!'

'Maybe I don't go either. It's just that it's very good for——'

'Don't miss your exercise on my account. I read somewhere that running doesn't really suit women anyway, they get stress fractures,' Bethany gave him as a parting shot, and left quickly before he could come up with some esoteric research to prove her wrong.

She went up to shower, and came down again wearing her shorts and bikini top, with an open shirt loosely slung over the top for decency. There was a quiet piece of garden well away from the main lawns, hedged for privacy too, and there was no reason why she couldn't go there without inviting Neil to come out and snarl at her for looking too feminine. It was a thought to be crushed quickly. It was also followed by the sour assumption that by now, no one would notice. Then, in contradiction, Lang looked up as she passed the sitting-room door and gave her a deliberate wolf-whistle.

'Oh, come off it, you know me too well by now! Go back to your *Theory of Surgery;* then when you're a Fellow and an ultra-rich consultant, you can afford a—a Rolls to garage with your Lamborghini!'

'I'll have a Ferrari and a Jensen, thanks!'

Bethany gave him a wave and went on out. He was right to occupy his time so usefully, and maybe she ought to do the same—revive her surgical ambitions and mug up for a further qualification, or perhaps do some extra studying on anaesthetics to push her career further in that field . . . The whole idea of her working future was suddenly remarkably dispiriting. The sweep of country down from the house seemed to hold a beauty to break the heart too, as it lay dreaming in the sun; even if its emptiness looked positively domestic after Canada . . .

She made her way round to her chosen piece of garden and spread her towel out in the middle of its smooth grassy sward. It was empty and quiet without even a window looking out this way, and the air was filled with the tantalising sweetness of the climbing roses which danced and nodded high up on a blank wall. Bethany stretched out and made a deliberate effort to blank her mind. She ought to be contented, out here in the sun: it ought to be giving her a feeling of luxurious ease to be lying here instead of scurrying round hospital wards and feeling envious of those who had time to acquire a tan.

She toasted her front, then rolled over after a while to do the same for her back. If she concentrated hard enough, surely she could imagine she was lying on a beach somewhere, with sand just beyond her finger-tips and palm trees gently swaying nearby. She would have to invent something for the scent the roses. It could be frangipani, whatever that was. And no, she *didn't* have sandflies plopping in to land on her back——

Something actually was landing on her back. Her head jerked up and she twisted round abruptly.

Neil was standing over her, carefully positioned so that she shouldn't feel his shadow, a tiny pebble poised between his outstretched fingers.

She looked up into the intense blue of his eyes and her heart gave a flip that seemed to bounce back off her lungs. Then she was sitting up rapidly, one hand rising to shade the dazzle of sunlight.

'This is an extremely private piece of garden, so *if* you're going to complain——'

'There's no need to sound so acid,' he said in a milder tone than he'd used for days. 'I'd noticed there was no one else here whose blood pressure you might raise!'

The deep voice with its mild teasing note was too much. Bethany struggled for a light flippancy, though it came out with an edge to it. 'No danger of that anywhere, I'd say—though if you *will* persist in worrying, I'm sure you could find a suitable bromide to prescribe out of the drug cupboards! Shall I recommend one?'

'Perhaps it would be a good idea. You're the expert!'

'I haven't noticed you being concerned about the effect on *me* of Erik's running shorts, or——'

'Stop picking a quarrel—though I suppose it's marginally better than the cool formality you've been offering me lately!'

'*That's* a good one! You've been snarling like——' Bethany broke off as, disconcertingly, Neil folded himself down to sit beside her in a rangily muscular movement. Her heart gave another thump and her widened eyes fixed themselves on the lean face turned towards her—until she forced herself to look away and down, pulling at a grassblade as if it held something suddenly to absorb her. 'Oh, all right, it's the work problems, I suppose,' she said in a carefully light voice, and added, since it came into her eyeline where he had placed it on the grass, 'I see you've brought the cordless telephone out with you, just in case!'

'It seemed a good idea to carry it with me on my walk around the gardens—unnecessary though it may be,' Neil added drily, and stretched. The movement, caught out of the corner of Bethany's eye, seemed to send a ripple through the air.

'It's difficult, isn't it? We'd like to work, but wishing for it is like wishing for someone to get hurt——' She knew she was talking for the sake of talking. 'There must be some sort of time limit on it. On letting us sit here if we aren't really necessary, I mean. Oh, I suppose you haven't heard how our Canadian patients are doing?'

'I checked, and they're all progressing. Lang's burn patients too. It shows we do have some point to our existence. Just for that, you can still your conscience and sit in the sun. I thought everyone was being conscious of ultra-violet these days, haven't you brought any sun oil out with you?'

'I haven't got any. I don't usually burn anyway——'

'No? Your skin's fair, even if you've got big dark eyes. Pity, that gives me no chance to offer to rub your cream on for you . . .'

The smooth deliberateness of the words sent warning bells jangling along Bethany's nerves. They set a tingle too which she tried to counter by stiffening her shoulders and shooting him a deliberately scathing look. 'Just to pass the time? Maybe you don't remember the old joke—"It would have passed anyway?" '

'To pass the time pleasantly. Do you really have so much against that?'

The blue of his eyes seemed to dazzle in the air between them. Bethany gulped and began to scramble to her feet.

'In the beginning I wasn't to be a temptation, I seem to remember. I'm really surprised that it doesn't worry you to be setting such a bad example as to—to *flirt,* and with a line that every crass idiot must have tried at some time on summer holidays throughout the world!'

'You don't have to react as if you'd been stung, do you?' Neil came to his feet himself and she thought there was an angry flash in his eyes, though his voice seemed to be trying for lightness. 'I haven't got two heads. I haven't committed any crimes—unless it's a crime to find you attractive. So do you have to stand there spitting at me like an angry kitten? No, all right, all right, I know you're a thoroughly competent surgeon and a good anaesthetist! But you're also——'

'Here and handy and fair game, because I know the score? That's——'

He closed the space between them in one step and grabbed her, his arms closing like a band of iron against her bare skin. One hand raised her chin with inexorable swiftness and his mouth came down on hers, hard and bruising, stinging her lips with the force of his own and sending shockwaves through her entire body. His grip moulded her against him so that she could feel the lean hardness of chest and hip and thigh with a potent sexuality and a radiating, melting warmth. He kissed her with a ferocity that deprived her of breath, of thought, of will, and lit her into a flaming response greater than any she had ever known . . .

Her lips were released to let him nuzzle her neck. It sent spirals of pleasure through her. She heard him murmur, very breathlessly, and with the tiniest edge of amusement, 'Hardly a bad example, sweet girl, in this *very* private place—and anyway, just at this moment, to hell with rules . . .'

The words seemed to wake her from a sensual dream. Her hands pushed against his chest: to her surprise, he instantly released her. She almost stumbled as she stepped back, so sharply that it was like wrenching herself away from warmth. Neil's releasing hands trailed against her bare arms with a sweet shiver which set the hairs rising on them. Her eyes found his face—the clean, lean lines of it, black eyebrows slightly raised, blue eyes deepened with passion—and she saw the way his lips were curved with satisfaction——

Bethany did the only think she could think of, and slapped his face.

It was a hefty slap with all the force of her arm behind it. The blood came up into his cheek in a red mark, and the unexpectedness sent him rocking back on his heels. She was pleased to see that disbelief wiped his face clean of expression.

'I told you I came here to *work!*'

Her voice sounded choked. She could only hope he would take it for nothing but anger. She *was* angry—not least with herself, for that betraying response her body must have given. Which he couldn't have helped but be aware of, and all the time they both knew there was Catherine . . .

She supposed he might have answered her if there hadn't been the most banal of interruptions. The telephone lying on the grass began a shrilling, insistent beep.

Neil bent to pick it up, and it was unreal to hear his voice sounding abrasively normal as he snapped his name. He listened for a moment, his eyes turning briefly to Bethany and away again. Then he spoke, with an icy curtness which ought to have made the person the other end blench.

'This is a private line, attached to an emergency radio link, and you shouldn't have been put through on it. No, you can't, and no, I haven't the least idea!'

He snapped the aerial back into place. His eyes came back to Bethany, levelly—but with ice in their depths, and a scathing coldness in his voice.

'That—again—was your friend Dr. McKinley. The

man in your life whom you summarily ditched in order to come here, if I read his messages right. I suggest, for the sake of all our peace, that you do something to sort the situation out—whatever the situation may be!'

'I didn't give him that number——'

'He got hold of it somehow, and doesn't seem deterred from trying it when he can't get you on the other. He doesn't seem to be able to take no for an answer, does he? Or was he foolish enough to believe you might keep your options open? Well, *as* we're not busy, you can take three days off and go down to Glasgow to sort the whole thing out!'

His look wouldn't allow her a denial. Pride wasn't going to let her tell him that she hadn't ditched Daniel, *he* had ditched *her,* whatever the situation now might be. She stared at Neil dumbly, seeing that the red mark was still visible, if fading, on his cheek. Pain and regret were suddenly tangling themselves into her emotions—a regret she certainly shouldn't be feeling. How could she, how could she possibly, when Catherine was someone she had truly liked? And knowing his relationship with the other girl, how *could* she have let Neil's touch, his lips, draw such an overwhelming response from her?

She turned abruptly and unsteadily on her heel, stooped to gather up her towel and discarded shirt, and swept out of the sunny, fragrant garden whose peace seemed to deny that it could ever have held a storm of emotion.

Neil's stinging iciness towards her must be the product of injured conceit—and surprise that she wasn't ripe to offer him casual amusement when he had assumed she would be. Men *were* obviously all the same. Anyone less naïve than she would obviously have learned that long ago.

In the circumstances she might just as well have settled for Daniel. In fact it would be the most logical thing to do—to go back and start again and remember how easy it was for a moth to singe its wings . . .

She had been given three days off, so she might as well go today. She would stop on the way to ring Daniel with a warning that she was coming, so that they could arrange somewhere to meet. Maybe if what Neil had told Catherine was true, and the job up here might be of an uncertain duration, she ought to be putting out feelers for other work anyway . . .

She had backed her car out of the garage and was just getting bask into it after closing the garage doors when Erik appeared. He was dressed in full-length trousers and a shirt and had a rucksack on one large shoulder. He was waving hopefully at her, so she paused.

'Bet'anee, Neil says you're going down to Glasgow and I may also have time off and go with you while I can get the lift. You don't mind? They can do without us, he says: unfortunately I think this seems true!'

'You're welcome to come. There isn't much leg room, though, I think you might be rather squashed——'

'It's all right. I can put the seat back so, see? I don't bring a car myself, I came up with a helicopter as a hitch.' Erik settled himself into the passenger seat with surprising ease, though he inevitably took up a lot of room. 'You look very nice,' he said approvingly, somewhat to her surprise. She was wearing a skirt for once, in a defiant red which almost matched the car, and had teamed it with a sleeveless white top.

'I decided I was tired of wearing trousers all the time. I usually have because there could be a call.' Also because she had deliberately chosen unisex attire. 'It makes a change,' she said with unnecessary forcefulness, and started the engine with a slightly too abrupt roar which had her reaching hastily to cancel the choke.

Erik was cheerfully companionable as they drove down through the Highland scenery. He told her about Sweden and about his medical school, which he seemed to have entered at seventeen, so he must be very bright. He didn't ask any questions when she stopped to make her telephone call. Daniel expressed delight that she was coming, though he sounded a little sore that it had taken her so long, a whole three weeks after their conversation. He said he could get off at five and that he'd meet her at the flat. There was somehow a comfort in the familiarity of his voice: this was a man she did at least know through and through—now—without room for misjudgements or surprises . . .

Rain had begun to sweep in, on a buffering wind, by the time they were approaching Glasgow. It slicked the grey streets and sent the crowds hurrying along the pavements.

'Our fine summer doesn't seem to have got this far,' Bethany commented lightly.

'It won't last up there either, I think. The weather forecast talked about storms travelling north. By the time we get back, it will probably have hit!'

'Oh?' That would be a change. The Highlands had had remarkably good weather up to now. 'I wonder what it's like for the helicopters in a rainstorm? Though the air-sea rescue ones go out in everything, don't they, so I suppose the pilots must be trained to cope with it!' An absent frown touched her brows as she threaded her way through the traffic. 'It did occur to me that Achnabrae might be a less than ideal choice in winter, because even if snow's all right, I'm sure they must get closed in by fog sometimes . . .'

'I too wonder, but maybe they have a plan for that?'

Or maybe not. It was an echo to suggest that Neil's theory might be correct.

She set Erik down on a street corner with arrangements as to where they would meet up for the return journey, and left him looking large, rapidly wet, but still unshakeably cheerful.

She ought to be feeling cheerful herself, with a reunion ahead of her. Anything else must only be the rain clouding her mood to grey.

CHAPTER ELEVEN

SHE COULD tell Daniel that she'd satisfied her sense of adventure with the private job now so was prepared to settle down. She would't wait for FTI's decisions, but he'd have to give her time to get out of her contract properly. She would also establish that in the future they'd have a relationship of mutual trust and sharing and that it *would* be marriage this time, a real one full of thoroughly-discussed future plans. The past would be over, for both of them, and the time ahead would be different.'

That seemed to cover everything, and Bethany climbed out of the car which she had managed to park opposite the small café two floors down under the flat. Rain drove down inside the collar of her hastily-donned jacket as she took a quick dash across the road. It was almost six, so Daniel would be there . . . She was lifting her hand to the bell on the closed lower door when someone darted out of the café doorway and tugged at her arm.

'Dr. Dale . . .'

The face peering urgently into hers was vaguely familiar, but the driving rain darkened the hair peeping out from under a headscarf and washed the pale cheeks into childishness. 'Yes?' Bethany began. The fingers pulling insistently at her sleeve suggested an emergency and she opened her mouth to explain that she wasn't a doctor at the hospital any more; but the girl was tumbling on with a breathless defiance.

'I've been waiting for you. He told me to get out because you were coming, so I hung around. *Please* listen to me before you see him!'

With a sudden clarity, Bethany knew who it was. The girl didn't look nearly as pretty in a mac and headscarf and with her face streaked with wetness which was—almost certainly—tears as well as rain; she certainly didn't look doll-like, more bedraggled; but it was definitely the staff nurse Daniel had moved out to live with. None other.

'I think we'd better go into the café.' Practicality seemed to take Bethany over. 'We can't talk out here in the rain. Come along—I'm sorry, I don't know your name.'

'Don't you? Didn't you ever bother to find out? It's Rachel.' The hostile first words stung, but there was a half-swallowed sob as she said her name. Poor girl . . . They reached the warm fug of the café's slightly grubby interior, and a waitress called out 'Two tassies, or two full teas?' with boredom and without bothering to move, as they sat down at a table covered with a red-checked oilcloth.

'Just the tassies, no food, thanks.' It was left to Bethany to answer, but they would have to take something as an excuse to be in here. The café was totally empty apart from them.

'Dr. Dale——'

'You'd better call me Bethany. I expect you know that's what it is. This place seems to have gone down-hill a bit, or am I just remembering it wrong? It used to do quite edible suppers.'

Bethany had only been talking to give Rachel the chance to recover from another gulp of tears, so she wasn't ready for the immediate hostile response.

'I do know, I was living upstairs until three weeks ago! As if it wasn't bad enough that he insisted we moved back into *your* flat, with *your* things in it——' She broke off as the waitress arrived to plonk two strong teas down in front of them and hold out her hand for fifty pence. Bethany paid her. As soon as they were alone again she took up the conversation in a surprisingly steady voice.

'You were living there until three weeks ago? I didn't know. Still, never mind that for the moment, what did you particularly want to say to me?'

'I'm pregnant,' Rachel said flatly. 'I thought you ought to know. I bet *he* won't tell you. He told me to have an abortion, but I said I wouldn't. I *want* his baby . . .'

'Did you decide to get pregnant on purpose?' Bethany asked politely. She didn't know how she was keeping so ice-cool; it seemed to be happening without her volition.

'All right, I did! I'm a nurse, after all, I'm not so likely to do it by accident, am I? I thought—I thought——Only when I told Daniel he was furious. He told me to have an obortion or move out. He made me move out, chucked all my things about, after I'd said——Oh, it just isn't *fair,* and I thought he'd be sure to change in the end! I thought it was just the shock, and lots of men don't think they want a baby in the beginning—and I thought he *loved* me . . .'

'Do you still love him? After that, I'd have thought *you* might have changed your mind! After all, getting pregnant does take two!'

'Don't patronise me!' the girl said furiously. Bethany wanted to tell her that she wasn't, she was only trying to adjust herself to what was being thrown at her. but the angry and tear-laden voice was going on. 'Then when I tried to get him to talk about it properly he said there was no point because *you* were coming back. And that I ought to have realised it was only temporary because everybody knew you and he . . . I didn't believe it at first, I thought he was only saying that, but then when I turned up at the flat tonight he said you were on your way right now and that was it. He was quite cool about it, he just said there was no point in letting me in and you were due to arrive any time!' She swallowed on bitterness, and on a kind of shock too; then she burst out, 'Oh, I was warned, lots of people tried to tell me!'

'Tried to tell you what? No, I'm *not* being patronising, I really want to know!'

'They told me about you and him and your open relationship, of course! That you knew what he got up to and didn't mind. And that it always gave him an excuse to move on. I didn't believe it,' Rachel said with a sudden desolation. 'He *didn't* seem like that . . . Anyway, you threw him out, didn't you, and went away? No one ever said it was just short-term— that you hadn't gone for ever!'

'Just tell me something. No, please, it's important. When *exactly* did he tell you I was going to come back? I mean, was it straight away——?'

'No . . . it was later. It was Sunday and I wasn't on duty, but we'd been arguing about the abortion again, and I went out for a walk because I was feeling so hurt. Then when I came back he'd bundled my things together and said I was to get out, and you were coming back.' Rachel gave her a look between anger, stubborness, and defensiveness. 'And it's not *fair*——'

'For me to walk in and out of his life? I'd agree with you—if that's what I was doing. *I'm not.*' Bethany studied the very young face in front of her, and the dawning doubt in it. 'I'm not coming back, no way, full stop. You—and he—can be absolutely sure of that! I've—I've just come down tonight to fetch some things. I'll say something else: from living with Daniel, I can tell you that he's charming and apparently lovable, but actually he's a rat and a bastard. It just takes a little while to find it out. OK? Now you've got a choice: you can go public and let everyone know you're pregnant—I suppose they don't?'

'No . . . He said if I told anyone he'd deny it and say it wasn't his——'

'Well then, as I said, you can let it go round and let public opinion shame him—which I guess he *wouldn't* like, because he's really quite vain, you know—in which case you *might* find he'll marry you. I wouldn't actually recommend that, because rats don't change and it'd be no fun being married to one. he'd just use you—the way he used me. I mean it, whatever you think! Anyway . . . I don't suppose you want my advice, or will listen to it, but if I were you I wouldn't touch him with a bargepole. And yes, I do know you've got some nasty alternatives. You're the only one who can actually decide about that. Now, I'm going upstairs to collect a few items I left behind——' a few items such as her illusions. No, those were already gone. 'After that I've no intention of going anywhere near him again,' Bethany finished, and pushed back her chair. 'All right?'

She would have liked to wish Rachel luck, but that probably wouldn't be taken well. She would have liked to say, grimly, that after the next ten minutes someone had better come and scrape Daniel off the walls. She didn't offer that for fear Rachel might still be so deluded as to want to. Instead she went outside into the cold rain and pressed her finger insistently on the doorbell.

His voice came tinnily through the answerphone and broke into glad relief when she said her name. *That* wouldn't last long!

He had to be unbelievably blind not to see the coldness in her face as he opened the upstairs door to her. Apparently he was. She had only had time to take in the smooth good looks, the dark trousers and plain white shirt, when he had swept her inside and into his arms.

'Beth . . . I was beginning to think you were never going to get here! Honey, I've missed you. Say you've missed me too—go on, I dare you, say it . . .'

There was a time when the feel of him would have weakened her and when being rocked in his arms would have warmed her with joy. Not now. She could examine her reactions clinically, and she merely felt smothered. 'Let me go, please,' she said with cool impatience—and didn't bother to push, simply waited with a rigid lack of reaction for him to comply. 'And do let's get it clear—I've only come because my boss sent me to sort things out, to stop you making all those phone calls!'

'Oh, Beth, c'mon . . .'

'No!' She evaded the lips that tried to kiss her, and something in her basilisk stare at last seemed to get through to Daniel and make his arms drop. It was interesting to see that he immediately put on his injured-little-boy look. And had she *really* never noticed the weakness of his mouth before? 'The game is very definitely up,' she said drily. 'I met your pregnant girlfriend downstairs.'

'Oh, hell, she's such a *nuisance*! And it's *not* my baby, if she told you it was. Goodness knows she puts it about enough, and I haven't had anything to do with her since just after you left, I told you! Darling, you don't believe——'

Bethany walked across the room, picked up the music centre, held it high, and let it drop on the floor. It fell with a satisfactorily shattering crash. Daniel's face turned white with shock and anger. *Good*!

'What the *hell*——That was a valuable piece of equipment!'

'I thought socialists didn't believe in property. Anyway, one of your messages said you didn't want it, I think. OK, now you haven't got it. Be warned, Daniel, I'm feeling *extremely* violent, even though I know perfectly well you aren't worth it! Why that poor girl downstairs wants to have your child I don't know——'

'You'd believe anything anybody said about me, wouldn't you? Anyway, I don't want kids, this isn't a world to bring them into—*if* it was mine, and you've only got her word for that!'

'She hasn't had much time to get pregnant by someone else in the last three weeks, has she? And she was living with you until then. Until just after you'd rung me up with honeyed words, to persuade me to come back and protect you from the consequences of your actions!'

'You think it was like that? I mean, you really *believe* that? Oh, come on, Beth, this isn't like you any more than throwing the furniture about is like you——' Daniel saw her hand move deliberately towards one of the pair of speakers and moved hastily between her and it. 'Darling, get it out of your system some other way, will you? And look, you're the only woman I want, you know that. I meant every word I said——'

'*Don't* try it. For once, I can see you really clearly!'

'If you hadn't chucked me out on a rumour none of this would have happened, did you think of that? God, if you could see the look on your face, you've turned so *hard,* I'd scarcely have recognised you! And there was I, missing you, wanting you, wanting all the old love and friendship we used to have——'

'I doubt if we were ever *friends,*' Bethany said coldly, and knew all at once it was true. Lovers, yes, with a bemused magic to switch off her mind and suspend all her critical faculties—but what else had they shared? Now she came to look at it, not even work—except for Daniel's frequent grumbles that this or that person had been putting him down, so that she could soothe him with her partisan support. The shattering even of memories seemed infinitely sad and she didn't know why she had come up here at all. Except to make it clear that they were finally, absolutely finished.

Daniel must have seen something in her eyes and taken it for a softening, because he move swiftly towards her. 'Ah, Beth, come on, let's forgive and forget. We belong together, you know we do! Darling, I know what you need. Let's go to bed, and make it up there——'

Her rapid evasion of his reaching arms, her look of outraged revulsion, finally seemed to get through to him. His hands dropped and a truly spiteful look came into his face to make its handsomeness ugly. 'Oh, I see what it really is—you've found someone else, haven't you? All this virtuous bit because I've got into a mess is just that, isn't it? Too-good-to-be-true Bethany—and now we see you in your true colours, don't we? Who is it? One of your fleshpots with plenty of money to splash around? Your pot-bellied boss, perhaps? I don't suppose you mind his figure when he earns a bomb and can spend it all on you!'

It was on the tip of her tongue to slash at him with the truth about where Neil spent his money, just to cut him down to size. Then she knew she wouldn't bother. She said wearily, 'Oh, shut up, Daniel, and stop being such a spoiled brat. That's what you really are, isn't it? And we have nothing else to say to each other—now, or ever.' Then she turned away, crossed the room, and walked out.

She had to hope for Rachel's sake that she wouldn't have him . . . but she didn't really care, either way. And that was almost the saddest thing of all.

She couldn't go back to Achnabrae without Erik, so she spent the next two days staying in a guesthouse the other side of Glasgow from the hospital. She could have gone and looked up Mark and Trisha and some of her other friends, but she didn't want to. It rained. She walked about through the wet streets. She had her hair cut again because it was something to do. She bought various medical journals, read through them meticulously, and checked their columns in case there were any interesting jobs on offer. There weren't, unless she could persuade someone that she'd be a suitable junior clinical assistant in the Seychelles. Finally, and just when the wind had blown the rain away to give an apology for returning summer, she went to pick Erik up from their prearranged rendezvous.

He was exuding health and good humour and politely told her, again, that she was looking very nice, which very nearly got him his head snapped off for his pains. He gave her a thoughtful look but was prudent enough to decide on silence. Bethany drove grimly through Glasgow's endless outskirts, putting her foot down whenever she got the chance and cutting corners wherever the opportunity presented itself, then put her foot down properly when they reached the end of the speed limit. She wasn't aware of anything but a savage pleasure in movement to ease pain, until Erik spoke abruptly as if the words were jerked out of him.

'Bet'anee, would you mind very much if I drive? You are upset, I think, and if you go on swerving round lorries I don't——Please pull over, I really do think it would be safer!'

She swung to the side of the road and slammed on the brakes. Then, to her extreme chagrin, she burst into tears.

She was aware some time later that Erik was holding her companionably against his large chest, patting her with his spare hand, and that he had lent her a very large handkerchief.

'I'm—I'm sorry . . .'

'It's all right. You need to cry, so you cry, ho?' He patted her again comfortingly, and she looked up at him out of a tearstained face.

'How *old* are you, Erik?'

'Me? I'm twenty-seven. And Lang's twenty-eight, and Peter thirty-one, I think. Does this have some point?'

'Just that you've no reason to be so *paternal*—but I'm grateful just the same! I wish I didn't feel a hundred and two . . .'

'While I'm paternal, do you want to talk about it?'

'Oh . . . it's just that the man I used to live with turns out to be someone I never would have loved if I'd really known him. That's probably the oldest story in the world!'

'Maybe you fall in love with someone else instead. It would make a good cure.'

She almost told him she'd tried that, but was a bad picker. That her tears were partly for that too—for her forced conclusion that men were all the same when you scratched the surface. That would hardly be polite to him, as he sat there so patiently weathering her emotions, so she didn't. She sat up instead and gave him a watery smile.

'Thanks for being nice, and I'm sorry again. And maybe you're right, and you *had* better drive, ho?'

'That's good, you're feeling better, so you tease me,' Erik said tranquilly, and smiled at her, looking endearingly large and placid. 'We'll change over now, and stop somewhere on the way so you can make your face. OK?'

They adjusted the driving seat to accommodate his vastly long legs and set off again at a more decorous speed. It was really quite peaceful being with Erik; not least because he was so thoroughly undangerous. And her storm of tears seemed to have accomplished one thing: they had washed Daniel totally out of her system. Even if not Neil . . .

She wasn't going to dwell on that thought, with the despair of knowing it was true, which made her a hopeless masochist. She particularly wasn't going to dwell on it as they finally swept up to Achnabrae, shrouded in the rain they had met in Glasgow and buffeted by an angry wind. After they'd garaged the car she let Erik pull her rapidly across the courtyard, which was filled with swirling rain, and they fell breathlessly into the house, shaking drops from their clothing.

'Ugh, it's not fair to meet a storm in two places! Hi, Pete, I suppose you haven't had any calls while we were gone? It might be quite hard to take off in this, anyway!'

'You haven't heard? No, I suppose it hasn't made the news bulletins yet. Lang and Neil have gone out . . .'

Bethany realised all at once that he was looking uncommonly grave. 'What?' she asked rapidly, feeling Erik stir beside her with the same unspoken question.

'The storm hit the North Sea really badly, and something broke on Rig Three. It sounds like a metal fracture in one of the legs. They've got several hurt. Neil didn't feel it was a job for an anaesthetist because they're evacuating everyone anyway, but he and Lang went along as doctors because there are people trapped. It wasn't going to be easy—they'd have to be dropped down instead of landing, and if they go inside I hope to God they get out again! It sounds as if the whole thing might go over . . .'

Bethany stared at him with the blood draining out of her cheeks, and her heart making a sickening turn in her chest.

Neil . . .

CHAPTER TWELVE

THERE WERE confused, nailbiting hours when it was difficult to know what was happening. The news services quickly picked up on the story and went into lurid prose where the words *disaster* and *tragedy* figured prominently. The pictures that flashed on the television screen certainly echoed the description; rain-lashed seas full of huge angry waves, hovering helicopters with lines dangling down from them, men in the water . . . There were shots of the rig at an ungainly tilt with one corner crumpled and spikes of metal spearing out at odd angles. There were further shots of lifeboats hurrying to the scene through the smash of heavy water. It was mentioned that the rig's owners, Forbes Travis International, were flying a bunch of top executives to Scotland at once. There was talk of a public inquiry.

What there wasn't, for hours, was the news Bethany was straining her ears to hear; that Neil was safe. And Lang too, she thought with hasty guilt.

Then suddenly the Achnabrae telephone started ringing, just as radio and television news were reporting 'the successfully completed evacuation of all the surviving crew members'. It was the newspapers seeking personal details about Lang, who was apparently being hailed as a hero. They'd got his name but they wanted his background; where was he from, what was his usual job, his age, his marital status? Peter had just finished fielding that with as little information as he could offer while trying to find out information of his own, when the internal phone gave its sharp buzz.

Bethany reached it first in a close contention with Erik. Her breathless acknowledgement brought the laconic voice of one of the radio operators.

'Message in to say both our docs are OK and will be on their way back when a 'copter's free. Thought you'd like to know!'

'*Thanks* . . . Neil and Lang are *both* safe,' she passed on. 'Apparently they're on their way back. Or will be as soon as they can get transport. That's— that's——'

'Great,' Peter said, and allowed his shoulders to relax for the first time in hours. Erik had seized hold of Bethany and was giving her an unexpected hug that lifted her right off her feet, though he put her down at once with a hasty look of apology. The general telephone in its room off the hall began another shrill ring and Peter began to move towards it, then stopped.

'I suggest we don't answer, it's probably another newspaper and I've already told them they'll have to get all their information from FTI. Well . . .' His face was split with a relieved grin, though there was a soberness behind his eyes for the news the television set was still giving out. Six crew members were reported dead, a possible further two were missing, and several were being transferred to the local hospital. It could have been even worse if the rig had gone over, but luckily it had stayed at its uneasy tilt—and as the weather was now abating, it was judged to be going to stay that way. 'So Neil and Lang are safe, that's good,' Peter brought out. 'I suppose we'll have to wait until they get here to find out exactly what the situation out there did throw at them! They certainly seem to have made themselves useful, anyway—if the press's sudden interest in Lang is anything to go by!'

'We'll read about it in tomorrow morning's papers if they don't return before then,' Erik put in. 'I guess everything's very busy still, so they may have to wait to come back, yes?'

Bethany hoped not. She knew she wouldn't truly believe Neil was in one piece until she actually saw him. As it turned out, however, it *was* morning before a salt-stained chopper came clattering in to the landing-pad on the lawn, deposited two familiar figures, and took off again about its business.

It was still only breakfast time, but her early rising had already gleaned some of the facts from a selection of newspapers brought up by a van with the post. It was the tabloids which had got on to Lang—with a picture too, slightly blurred but recognisable and apparently landing on the mainland with a stretcher case. From the story and diagrams, it appeared that he had been lowered down into the most dangerous area of crushed wreckage and had helped to bring up two survivors. There were purple passages of prose with the phrases, 'into the jaws of hell . . .' and 'careless of his own safety, young New Zealand surgeon Lang Graham . . .'

As Bethany and Erik and Peter arrived simultaneously to form a welcoming committee, the sound of

Lang's careless tones met them.

'I wouldn't mind having lost them so much if they weren't positively my *best* boots, the ones I'd got thoroughly broken in!'

'Put in a chit to FTI for a new pair—and bump the price up,' Neil's deep voice answered with an equal lightness. 'Come to that, I don't think *my* footwear's likely to be much good after such a thorough soaking! Ah, people—what, all three of you? No other calls while we've been gone?'

He sounded, and looked, so normal that Bethany wanted to burst into tears. She restrained herself from doing anything so ridiculous, but how *could* he ask so coolly whether there'd been any other call-outs? She wrenched her eyes away from their tendency to dwell on every detail of his face and looked at Lang instead. He had scratches down one cheek and on both his hands.

'You seem to have been in the wars a bit—but then I've just been reading all about you in the paper——'

'It looked like a fairly dangerous manoeuvre you had to do,' Erik put in, a touch of envy in his voice.

'Oh, God, don't say the press have turned *that* into a lurid drama? I hope they're not going to turn up here!'

'They'd better not. Still, Erik can always stand at the front door looking very large and very blank and refuse to let anyone in. That's an official request, Erik, OK? I think I'll just go and make sure they're keeping our phone lines clear—and then I'm going to have a shower and a proper shave. While I'm doing that, Peter, you can stay in charge, all right?'

With that string of orders Neil left them, striding away rapidly. He was, very definitely, in one piece; he was his same abrasive, vigorous self. Bethany's heart turned over, a fact which she acknowledged despairingly but without trying to deny it. She was, quite simply, stuck with it.

Peter and Erik were plying Lang with questions and one of them had produced a newspaper to show him. The coverage drew forth an unprintable word and a look of disgust from Lang, with no attempt to pretend his usual casualness.

'Why do they have to build it up into such a story? And if they *must* do that, they might at least give proper credit to the right people! There's nothing here about the guys who had to get me in, and haul all of us out . . . They don't even bother to mention that Neil was going to go down if his shoulders hadn't been too wide for the space, either; *nor* the fact that he was dropped down off another rope into the sea to help with the survivors there!'

'*Was* he?'

'Sure was, and I'd have called that a lot worse, with the undercurrent threatening to smash everyone into the legs the whole time! I hope they give the 'copter pilots and the lifeboatmen medals, all of them—they certainly deserve it! The rig sub-foreman and his bunch ought to get a bravery award too: they had the job of stopping the drill and getting the bore capped with everything at sixes and sevens, and they got it done against appalling difficulties too!'

He revealed a moment later that the chief rig foreman had been one of the fatalities. Bethany remembered the man from her trips to Rig Three and felt a quick mourning regret. She hadn't known him at all well, but he had been solid and tough and practical and had treated her with courtesy. It was a bad business all round; an accident which should never have been able to happen, as FTI's public statements repeatedly said.

It was later when she managed to run into Neil. Somehow she had to, haunting the corridors on a variety of excuses until they actually came across each other in an empty passageway. He paused at the sight of her.

'Are you down here checking the drug cupboards? I think you'll find there's still plenty of everything, Peter went through your side of things only the other day!'

'Did he? I didn't know, and I had a sudden feeling we might be low on tubo-curanine.' The politely impersonal look he was giving her wasn't promising, and struck into her with an involuntary feeling of pain. She tried to sound no more than casually interested as she added, 'Lang's been telling us what you did. I suppose you're all right, are you?'

'A thorough soaking isn't actually going to do me any harm.' Before Bethany could open her mouth to protest at this description of his part in things he was going on, with a polite lift of one black eyebrow and a hint of sarcasm coming to touch his eyes. 'And you—did you manage to sort out your problematical love life while you were away? I hadn't forgotten, and in the circumstances it seems fair to ask whether you're thinking of leaving!'

'No.'

'Just like that? Or are we going to have more phone calls from this poor unfortunate you ditched out of a preference for your career?'

Bethany's temper suddenly went into overdrive. There had been too many drains on her emotions in the past few days; too much in too short a time. 'Just for the record,' she said between her teeth, 'he's a long way from being unfortunate, except in character, and *he* did the ditching! That happened before I came here. It may have been the *reason* why I decided to come here—quite apart from liking the sound of the job—but if anyone got abandoned, it was me! Not that I'm asking for your sympathy, I'm just sick and tired of hearing you make assumptions without bothering to find out if there are any grounds for them!'

'From his messages, anyone could be forgiven for drawing the wrong conclusion!'

'Well, now you know better, don't you? It may be common practice,' said Bethany, with a lift of her chin and a totally inimical glare, 'but *I* don't go round playing with other people's emotions!'

She turned and swept away from him with a speed which had taken her round the corner before he could answer her—if he had been going to answer her. She hoped her final shaft had struck home. It should have done. Neil would have to be very stupid not to know what she was referring to . . . and he wasn't stupid. As unprincipled as most attractive men seemed to be, perhaps, unless she was just a born victim; but no one who had worked with him would take him for a fool.

She was the only one who was a fool, to feel his magnetism in spite of everything, and churn inside with a hopeless, longing wistfulness which kept insisting that things *ought* to be different. That he wasn't really the kind to be two-faced; that the thread she could feel between them ran both ways and *was* more than attraction; that he was a man she could truly love . . .

She got upstairs to find a letter for her that must have gone unnoticed in her eagerness to scan the newspapers. Someone had slipped it under the door of her flat. She reached down to pick it up, wondering absently who it could be from when she didn't recognise the writing. Then she slit it open and, with irony, discovered who. Catherine.

It was a card rather than a letter; a postcard-sized photograph of the small prefabricated church at Marker Lake with a message on the back in neat rounded script. She could almost hear the Canadian nurse's soft friendly voice in the written words.

'Hi, Bethany! By the time you get this I'll be packing up to leave, but I'll send it down on the supply plane for posting. It was lovely to see you, and I hope we'll meet again one of these days. Take care, and God bless! Catherine.'

Nothing more than that—but it was reminder enough, if she had needed one. And Catherine was leaving . . . going to some more accessible place, presumably, to do some other nursing job, until such time as Neil could join her, or she him.

Bethany propped the photograph up on visible display beside the carving of the baby seals. Then she went down to lunch, when lunch-time came, and initiated a long and absorbing discussion with Peter on anaesthetics which took up the whole meal. It didn't make any difference, really, because Neil didn't appear. Someone said he was busy sorting some things out in his office over a plate of sandwiches.

He appeared for supper in the evening, but by the time he arrived the others were in the middle of teasing Lang for his sudden fame, and when that palled, there was a lively discussion between Erik and Lang on mountaineering techniques. It wasn't imagination to feel there was a loom in the air of faint discontent, release of tension after the call-out, concern for the casualties and fatalities, but frustration because call-outs were so infrequent. FTI executives were apparently gathering in Aberdeen but had made no contact with Achnabrae. It was almost possible to sense everyone wondering whether they would decide to rationalise the accident service while they were here. No one said anything out loud, but one could feel what they were thinking, behind a spate of carefully cheerful conversation.

When the evening finally broke up Bethany went to bed and lay there wondering what she was going to do with her life next. She really couldn't tolerate many more evenings like tonight, spent rigidly avoiding looking at Neil, occupying herself in empty shop-talk, challenging Erik to a snooker match which ended up with Lang and Peter coaching one side each because neither of the protagonists had played before . . . It was simply too *tiring,* let alone pointless! There was really nothing here to hold her any more. Nothing that *should* hold her. It wasn't even an escape from Daniel now—and leaving *would* be an escape . . . She had got that far, restlessly, when her door suddenly opened.

Erik came into the room and closed the door carefully behind him. He was wearing a short towelling dressing-gown that showed the usual expanse of vast Scandinavian leg, this time ending in large and very clean bare feet. He stood still for a moment, his head tilted slightly on one side.

'I saw you still have your light on. You're reading?'

'Oh . . . yes, I wasn't feeling particularly sleepy.' Bethany had really kept the light on so that Catherine's card could sit reprovingly in her eyeline. 'What is it, Erik? Something I can do for you?'

'We maybe talk for a while?' He came across the room, for some reason less muscularly balanced than usual, to judge from the fact that his foot caught a small coffee-table as he passed. It went over with a thump and he made a muffled exclamation, then bent to right it with care. 'Sorry, that was clumsy. You don't mind that I come?'

'Well, it's late. But——'

'I'm thinking about the other day,' Erik said, sitting on the end of her bed beside her feet. There was something not quite as placid as usual about him, and Bethany reached for her dressing-gown, meaning to sit up encouragingly so that he could tell her what was bothering him. Then, to her startled surprise, she found her hand caught and held.

'When you were crying, you know, and I told you to fall in love with someone else? You know that I find you very attractive, Bet'anee . . . No, don't say anything, but you remember when we worked together that time? In Greenland? Well, when two people work very well together it makes a bond. It also shows that they will be very good together in other ways——'

'Erik——'

'I don't think you should really sound so surprised. We do a lot together lately. I think you see how much I like you. If you let me stay with you I think it can be very good.' He was stroking her hand persuasively. He didn't seem to notice when the heavy book she had been trying to convince herself to read slid to the floor with another thump. 'Maybe you soon forget this other useless fellow——'

'Erik,' Bethany said again, desperately trying to pull herself together. She tried to release her hand too, but he wasn't having any of that. He was looking very large and singularly determined. She swallowed hard. 'Look, I'm——The company has a thing against relationships and——'

'So what will they know? Anyway, they don't organise very well and give us not enough to do. No, I don't mean that, now you think I just——' Erik slapped his other hand against his forehead; unfortunately he followed that up by bringing the hand down to reach out and stroke her cheek, at the same time shifting up closer to her. 'Bet'anee, you know I find you most attractive, and I don't just pass by and go away again. That isn't the way I am. We start out by liking each other a lot and see how it goes, why not? You'll forget that other man——'

'I already have. I mean, I—I don't need comforting, Erik, that piece of my past really is all over, and you were—were a tremendous help. But there are other——'

'We can be good together and start fresh then. You aren't in love any more, that's fine!'

His look of optimism wasn't fine at all, and she was trying to find enough breath to tell him that she was very flattered, *but,* when a tap come on her door. For a hysterical moment she visualised the equally unlikely figure of Peter arriving to make her a similar offer after never showing any sexual interest in her at all. Not Lang, because he *had* put out a mild early challenge and then calmed down . . . Then the door opened abruptly, and it was the last person she wanted to see—with Erik sitting on her bed in a meaningful manner in his very abbreviated dressing gown.

Everything seemed to go very still as she met a pair of vivid blue eyes that cast a comprehensive look into the room and then developed ice-chips. Erik had at least let her go abruptly at the arrival of a third party. He hadn't moved otherwise, though; and Neil's deep voice spoke promptly and with an extreme dryness.

'My apologies! I sleep just below and I thought there must be something wrong up here after hearing a couple of loud bumps . . . But I was obviously wrong! Erik, I *assume* you're in here by invitation——'

'It would be up to Bethany to say whether this is so or not,' Erik stated in a fit of what he appeared to see as chivalry. He stood up, all six foot five of him. 'But if you wish to know, we talk only! If you wish to make an issue out of it——'

'Not at all—now I've reassured myself that no one on my staff's had a sudden heart attack or set a room on fire. My apologies again, and goodnight!'

He was gone, the door closing behind him with a firm snap that seemed to echo the sarcasm in his voice. Before Erik could move Bethany was out of bed, wrapping her dressing-gown round her, making for the door in a sudden desperate need to tell him it *wasn't what he thought*—and then she stopped, her flight abruptly halted by the sick knowledge that it didn't matter anyway. He wasn't hers. He was Catherine's.

'Oh, I'm sorry. Will this make trouble for you . . .?'

She was aware suddenly that Erik was looking down into her face with his brow creased up like an anxious Great Dane puppy.

'It doesn't matter. It's not his business! I sometimes think that he carried on like the Thought Police, anyway, about other people's lives!' Bethany gulped, knowing abruptly that she sounded too bitter; too much as if she cared what Neil thought or did or might say. 'Look, Erik, I'm—I'm really very—very touched, and flattered, and—I like you tremendously, but I was going to say no anyway! I don't—I mean I'm not——'

'I see. I've been a little bit stupid, I think.'

'No! It's just that I never thought, and—if *you* thought I was encouraging you, I——'

'No, I *mean* that I've been stupid. I didn't see. You have a very readable face just now,' Erik said gently.

'I don't! It's easy to read people's expressions the wrong way——'

'Not a look like you gave to the door after Neil shut it. And the way you were worried while he was out on a dangerous job at the rig. Did you know how you looked then? It was too much for just a colleague—and I've seen you with Lang, so I know it wasn't for him!' He touched her shoulder gently but with no invitation at all now. 'You want me to try to explain to him——?'

'*No!*'

'OK. What do I say now—I'm sorry I bothered you?'

'Erik . . .'

'It's all right.' His cheerfulness suddenly came back. 'I'll just run an extra mile tomorrow—unless we get a call-out—ho?'

His extraordinary readjustment to placidity defused Bethany's attempt at apology. All the same, she began, 'Erik, I'm truly sorry . . .'

'I know when I'm beat,' he said with a grin. It was a grin which didn't seem to carry hurt feelings, remarkably. 'I go now. I go very noisily, too, for the benefit of people who sleep downstairs! You know, I'd say *he* was jealous too, so you don't need to look as if the world's ending. It means you can tell him I was only making you unasked-for offers and that you didn't co-operate! Goodnight, Bet'anee . . .'

He went—noisily. It was comforting that he didn't seem to care *that* much about being turned down. It probably wasn't important that she hadn't made him promise to say nothing, to anybody, either: he seemed remarkably good at keeping his own counsel. At hiding his feelings altogether . . . Or was she really still thoroughly blind and naïve in *all* her dealings with men?

It would appear so; she had certainly misread Erik!

It wouldn't do Neil any harm to think she could fancy someone else.

She countered the rebellious pain of that by walking to pick up Catherine's card, making herself read it; then she picked up the narwhal's tusk carving and rubbed it gently between her fingers. Bitter acknowledgements perhaps—and she would keep the little carving for ever—but it looked as if that would be her only memento of her time here.

Unless, of course, she changed her mind, and opted for large Scandinavian niceness, and ran off with Erik. It would probably be the wisest thing she could do, at that.

CHAPTER THIRTEEN

BETHANY HAD wondered if Neil would say something sarcastic—whether he would even have the nerve to call her in and haul her over the coals for being 'distracting' to the peace of the team. Could he even sack her? Well, that would at least take all decisions out of her hands; and give her something open and specific to answer to, too!

What she hadn't expected was that everything would go on exactly the same.

Erik exercised in the gym or went out running; Lang had an attack of devotion to his car and took parts of it to pieces; Peter read one of the German books he was often deep in; and Neil appeared at meals to be impersonally pleasant but spent the rest of the time out of sight.

There was even a call-out, to one of the other rigs. He sent Erik and Peter to deal with the fractured ankle. While they were gone he buzzed for Lang and the two of them spent a long time closeted in Neil's office: presumably they were making out a proper report on the casualties at Rig Three.

Bethany stormed inwardly with the frustration of having nothing to do. She was tempted to go out and drive—and then realised that she couldn't until Peter came back, just in case. It wouldn't do if they had another call-out that needed an anaesthetist.

It was even more frustrating when they didn't, and she was reduced to watching afternoon soap operas which seemed mainly to contain Australian doctors and nurses leading seething love-lives.

The head of tension she had built up sent her out defiantly as soon as Peter did come back. She thought Erik gave her a concerned look—perhaps he had gone back to being paternal, if of course he had ever felt that way—but she didn't attempt to tell anyone where she was going, merely left a message in the hall to say she was OUT. She drove for miles, grimly ignoring the outstanding scenery which had struck her so much on her way here; she drove until she reached the nearest sizeable town, then parked and made her way to the public library.

All the quality newspapers were on offer, so were some of the medical magazines. Bethany went through all of them with the thoroughness of somebody wielding a fine-tooth comb. She copied down the application addresses for even the most unlikely jobs. She also noted the telephone numbers of various medical agencies.

At least—and at last!—she was doing something *practical*. And if it came like a sour thought that she had just wasted several months of her working life, it wasn't all a waste, because it would look good on her CV. For a moment she was caught by the ironic idea of requesting Neil for a reference. If he had any sense of justice he'd have to give her a good professional one . . . and *if* he had any sense of justice, he wouldn't let anything personal colour it!

She wouldn't ask him, though. She'd just quote

FTI as her last employer.

It all seemed thoroughly lined up. There wasn't actually any job going which would send her rushing to put pen to paper—but there *was* always locum work. She'd try the south of England perhaps, maybe even London. She left the library as it was closing and managed to find a stationers, where she bought a pad and some envelopes. Then she set off for the drive back to Achnabrae.

The Manor looked as impressively elegant as ever and the stormy weather, blowing itself out as fast as it had risen, had left a clear-washed sky of a pale egg-shell green. Bethany spared no look for that or for the varied blues of the distant hills and walked into the house with a decisive step. She heard Peter's voice in the sitting-room and paused to put her head round the door.

'*No* more call-outs, I suppose . . . ?'

'No, we're idle again.' It was Lang who answered her. 'Neil's just been called down to Edinburgh, though. He took off a few moments ago.'

'Edinburgh?'

'The FTI conference seems to have moved to there. Or maybe it's just where the big guns are staying—the summons came from Travis himself, we gathered.'

'The big chief? Oh, then maybe he'll come up here and tell us just what we *are* all supposed to be doing, instead of being paid to do nothing!'

'He could be giving praise where it's due after the rig incident,' Peter put in mildly. 'And for some of the other calls we actually have done. I don't really know how they view the economics. It *hasn't* seemed exactly practical so far, we've all been aware of that—but we'll just have to wait and see what happens after Neil's raised various points with him, won't we?'

Bethany didn't feel inclined to voice the suggestion she had learned from Catherine. It was a confidence she hadn't been supposed to share. She thought Lang had given Peter a slightly cynical look, so maybe the idea had been discussed with him too, as Neil's official second-in-command in this small community. She went away upstairs feeling determinedly that it had stopped being any of her affair. She was going to quit anyway. The sooner the better. In fact she would christen her new writing pad with a letter of resignation. It didn't matter that Neil wasn't here; he would hardly object, and telling him first was merely an unnecessary courtesy!

It was a relief that he wasn't in the house anyway. When he wasn't here it was *much* easier to forget the persistent, mistaken ache which her heart seemed to insist on giving. Perhaps, with luck, he'd stay away several days . . .

He didn't. He was back an hour after lunch-time the next day. Bethany had achieved a pile of brief official letters by then—job applications and enquiries and her resignation on the top of the pile—but she'd forgotten about stamps, and a drive to the village had brought the annoyance of finding the post office on a half-day closing. So was everything else, so she couldn't even buy the bar of chocolate which some inner need for comfort seemed to be urging her to want. She had just returned when the noise of a heli-copter set them all glancing at the windows. Then a moment later a lean wide-shouldered figure was in the doorway and glancing round at all of them with that intensely blue gaze.

'You're all here—good. I've got a lot to say, but would you mind if I see you one by one? Sorry if that sounds official, but it is. Lang, we've already discussed some of this, but will you come first? We'll go to my office.'

'Well, this is something definite, anyway.' Erik broke the silence left behind by the two men's departure. He gave Bethany one of his cheerful looks and seated himself in the nearest armchair. 'We see now. It's rather like the interviews all over again, isn't it? But this time shall we say Ladies First, and let Bet'anee go next?'

It seemed Neil had other ideas. When Lang came back he put his head round the door and said, 'OK, Pete?' and then went away, his footsteps retreating up the stairs. Bethany and Erik sat in silence. She knew he was shooting thoughtful glances at her, but she hid behind a newspaper, a clenching feeling in her stomach making her disinclined to chatter brightly or share curiosity. She *wasn't* curious, anyway. She really didn't care what Neil had to say to each of them. In her case they could have the briefest possible interview . . .

Peter came quietly back looking deadpan, paused in the doorway as Lang had done, and said, 'Erik? He wants you next.'

'Go ahead,' Bethany said swiftly as Erik hesitated. 'There's really *no* reason to keep him waiting!'

'OK. You know, Bet'anee, if——'

'Go and see what the big bosses had to say, go on! I'm not much interested anyway!'

He left her; alone, since Peter had departed too. This was getting like Ten Green Bottles, Bethany thought sourly. Why couldn't Neil have talked to them all together? If they *were* having their contracts terminated it applied to all of them, and doing it this way seemed an unnecessary drama.

It really was rather like the original interview to be sitting here waiting for Erik to come back. Her mind flew back to that time, to her first sight of Neil. What had she actually thought then? It was difficult to disentangle the past from the present; first impressions from the magnetism and magic and disillusionment since . . .

'Bet'anee?'

She jumped to find that Erik had come back. He had either arrived too quietly for her to notice or she had been miles away. 'My turn now, is it?' she said with a false brightness, and came to her feet. 'I suppose you're not going to say what——?'

'Only that it's going to be different. For you too, I hope—and whatever you want, I hope. And maybe we run across each other again some time. Without making misunderstandings!' Erik tacked on hastily, but with no reproach, only his usual happy cheerfulness. Then he made a shooing motion to send her past him and put a finger against his nose in what seemed to be a gesture of secrecy, smiling at her affectionately. He really was nice-natured; it was a pity that she . . .

She left that thought unfinished and concentrated instead on what he had given away. The Achnabrae accident unit obviously *was* being broken up. Well, it didn't matter to her either way. Her resignation might not be posted yet, but it was written. She set her face into a cool blankness as she reached the open door of Neil's office.

She had to crush the wistful pang within her as she saw him standing on the far side of the desk, his head turned to gaze out of the window beside him and the light edging his strong profile into planes and angles. He hadn't heard her arrival, so she could draw in the look of him, the uncharacteristically formal clothes of slacks and a jacket with a plain white shirt and a tie, when here he had often been in jeans and a T-shirt. Or flying overalls. Or a thick, rubbed, obviously well-used leather jacket, with a fur collar turned up around his face as leaned across her to point out the view of tundra lakes and meadows while they flew steadily across the Barren Grounds . . .

She stifled that particular memory sharply and stepped into the room, a trim figure in a bright yellow blouse and a beige skirt with a matching jacket slung round her shoulders. She had deliberately abandoned trousers for the last two days, almost like an assertion that she could be who she was and everyone could get used to it. As Neil turned to face her she squared her shoulders and widened her eyes into a look of polite enquiry.

'We seem to have arrived at my turn?'

'Yes. I've been given the job of telling everybody that Achnabrae's going to be closed down as far as we're concerned—sold off to be made into a nursing home, in fact. Your contracts——'

'You don't have to worry about mine, I'm resigning anyway.'

'Oh? That's just as well. I've pushed as hard as I can, but they persisted in regarding you as "an experiment" and don't feel there's really any other place for a woman doctor. I'm sorry about that——'

'Are you?'

'Naturally, so don't make it harder! You'll get a lump sum in lieu, of course.'

'I don't know if they really owe me that——'

'They do, so take it. I pointed out that you've done an excellent job whenever you got the chance. Unfortunately the way things are being reorganised there isn't an obvious place for you——'

'They are being reorganised, then? There's still going to be an accident team?'

'Yes, in a sense. I had some suspicions which may or may not have been justified, but by the time I'd put in a few words of my own, there's still contract work for the others. I did point out that if they terminated Lang's, for instance, they could easily find themselves with more headlines—"Hero doctor sacked", with all the outrage the press can produce on such occasions!'

In spite of his official manner Bethany let out an involuntary and appreciative chuckle. 'Did you really threaten them with that? And did Lang let you? After all his comments!'

'I didn't actually threaten, I just pointed it out, and I didn't ask him. I knew he wanted to go on with accident work and it seemed a good way to ensure it.' Neil's eyes seemed to be studying her face with an unusual intensity. Then his face was shuttered and impersonal again. 'We've all seen it coming. That we seemed to have been set up without proper thought, I mean, in view of the amount of work and the distances and so on. If we were just meant to be a loss-making exercise it certainly wasn't satisfactory from our point of view. Anyway, what they're doing now—after I'd made my points—is attaching one accident surgeon to each area and placing them reasonably close to that area. They agreed to one anaesthetist too, but I'm afraid that's Peter. He and Erik have been offered FTI's South American sites. Lang had already told me he was keen to work in Canada again, he seemed to have taken to it. So he's going there. The rigs are going back to being dealt with locally as they were before, so that's that.'

'And you?' Bethany asked involuntarily.

'I'm out—like you.'

For choice—for the freedom to marry Catherine. Because the name was in her mind it came to her lips. 'I had a card from Catherine,' she said with a forced brightness. 'She said she was leaving Marker Lake...'

'Yes, she's been recalled. It was abut time, I suppose. She'll miss it when it's been so much of her life, but she was looking on the bright side and saying there were advantages to Montreal.'

'And is that where you're going?'

'Me? No, why should I?' There was the flash of something in his eyes; then he said deliberately, 'Maybe I didn't need to tell you where Erik was going. He had time to tell you himself before you came along here!'

'There's nothing between Erik and me. Just because

two people talk to each other——'

'In the middle of the night? And extremely scantily dressed? He did make a rather heavy-handed point of telling me just now that I'd misunderstood his presence in your room, but——'

'I don't know why he bothered when you prefer your own opinion anyway! I told him not to—that it wasn't your business——'

'And you "don't play with other people's emotions"?' The official, impersonal discussion they had started out with had disintegrated with a rapid rise in temperature. 'I can't decide about you. At first I thought it must be something in what Cathy told you at Marker Lake. Then it seemed to be your determination to consider nothing but your career, which *certainly* fitted in with this McKinley character. Then I discover you're calmly carrying on with Erik! Do you *always* go around creating mayhem?'

'I was *not* carrying on with Erik! And I'm not responsible for his mistaken ideas——'

Bethany could have cut out her tongue for giving that away. Neil's eyes seemed to focus with an intensity of blue, and the thought of what he might say next brought her on to the attack, stung into angry words.

'What do *you* imagine I ought to be? A temporary entertainment for *you* once you've played fair, by your terms, by showing me who you're really in love with? Thanks a whole lot, that really makes things clear, doesn't it! And you have the *nerve* to assume that it's all just because I'm career-minded and not a human being at all! Just as if——'

'Wait a minute!' His sharp words stopped her.

'You're going to have to back-track! *What* was all that about "who I'm really in love with"?'

'Oh, don't be so ridiculous! As if I couldn't see what the situation was between you and Catherine! And I was meant to, wasn't I? Or why did you take me there? It isn't even a new twist,' Bethany said with bitterness, her mind flying to Daniel and the "open relationship" she was supposed to have had, 'though I must say it's more barefaced than most!'

Neil was standing so still that he might have been a statue. There was a blank surprise in his face which was either real or very good acting. "Me and *Catherine?*" he said, as if her words didn't make sense. 'Are you crazy, or just insulting? Not the latter, I hope, when you know perfectly well what she is!'

'Your cousin-in-law—yes, she told me. And I'm sorry about your wife, I can imagine how terrible that was for you.' Bethany didn't know why that had to come out in the middle of all this, but the words came by themselves. 'That's not the point now, surely? I mean, yes, she *was* someone you knew through your wife, but she's a lot more than that to you now! And she's beautiful and *good,* and I simply cannot take that you'd be prepared to treat her like that!'

Neil was still looking bewildered. Confused too, with an angry edge to it. 'Yes, she is beautiful and good—but if you know that, how can you think there could be anything between us? Except friendship? I suppose I *might* have fallen in love with her after the way she put me back together again; as it happened it didn't occur to me because I've always known her situation. That was already true when Sarah and I got married, so I've never . . . Are you saying that what turned you off me so abruptly—and apparently so thoroughly—was the fact that you got the impossible idea that I was paired up with *Cathy?*'

'Why—why not?'

'For one extremely obvious reason! Because she's a nun!'

Bethany felt as if someone had blown a hole right through her. She knew she was gaping. Neil stared at her, the vivid blue of his eyes a pattern of disbelief.

'You can't not have known! No, of course you knew—I told you when I introduced her! I remember, I said distinctly, 'Catherine's a nursing Sister——' he stopped. Then suddenly his shoulders began to shake, just as if there was something actually to *laugh* at. 'Oh no, I *see* . . . I'm so used to it, it's the way she says it herself, but you heard it the other way! You thought I said not nursing *Sister,* but *nursing* Sister!'

'It was the obvious way to hear it!'

'Not to me. We . . . ell . . . You did develop a bad opinion of my character, didn't you?'

'She doesn't look in the least like a nun!' Bethany managed, rallying. 'She doesn't dress like one!'

'She belongs to a very modern order. Anyway, they'd hardly expect her to wear robes in the Arctic! I gather they do wear them when they go into retreat. If she's back in Montreal by now I'd imagine she's all done up like that now, bless her. She knew she wanted to be a nun from quite an early age—in fact she started her novitiate before she did her nursing.' Neil paused, and Bethany felt a sense of hypnosis as he studied her across the room, his eyes raking her with a deep blue and apparently fascinated gaze. There was just the beginning of a smile curling the edges of his mouth. 'You may well blush, after jumping to conclusions just as badly as I do!'

'I seem to have——I just—you neither of you said anything that——You just seemed so thoroughly *together!*'

'We know each other very well. Or as well as two *friends* can. Other things are different.' He went on looking at her, but there was a sudden hesitancy about him. 'I asked her to tell you about Sarah. I suppose I thought at first that there was something in that to—I don't know, shock you, put you off——'

'No, how could there be? Of course there wasn't!' She couldn't bear that he might think so. 'Look, it was just a *misunderstanding*——'

'We seem to have a lot of those. I still can't quite take in that you thought she and I . . . And that was it, was it? Just that? Why you—switched off so sharply?'

'You can't say *just* that,' Bethany retorted—but breathlessly because of the dawning glow in a pair of sapphire eyes. 'I liked her so much, and I certainly wasn't going to——'

'Fall into the arms of a philanderer?'

'Fall into the arms of a philanderer *again*. I've been there once. Finding him out was what finished it. And yes, I *am* talking about the person you refer to as "this McKinley character"?'

'That makes things a bit clearer. It left you with a backlog of distrust, is that it? And the ability to assume all men were self-serving bastards? It's not an identity I've ever been accused of before, though there's really no way to give you *references* . . .' The dawning smile on Neil's face was doing disastrous things to her blood pressure. 'There is just one more thing I'd like to have *thoroughly* cleared up, and that's Erik . .'

'I wasn't falling into Erik's arms either. He just turned up and took me by surprise. Right up until then I'd thought he never even *noticed* women!'

'Oh dear, oh dear, you and your lack of belief in your ability to distract! Didn't I warn you? I must have been able to see even then how you were going to distract *me*.' There was open laughter in his face now but something more too; a gleaming, loving hope. 'Bethany . . . just tell me now, because I can't take much more of this! If I were to walk across the room and grab you and kiss you until your bones squeak, *would* you slap my face this time?'

'No . . .'

He could hardly have heard the word, but the look in her eyes must have answered him. He had reached her in two strides and his arms caught her against him with the same crushing, magnetic force she had felt last time. This time, though, there was no sense of ferocity or anger but a sweetness that parted her lips and sent her arms up round his neck with something which was almost, but not quite, a sob. Her response was total, all guards gone as she melted into him in a flame of passion which shook her to the roots of her being. But more than passion, more than a physical answer; her heart and spirit seemed to meld with his too . . .

'Oh, sweet girl, you *know* what we have between

us!' Neil's voice was deep and ragged against her ear. Then he put her away from him just a little to look down into her face. 'I never intended to fall in love with you, but it must have started happening right from the beginning. You with your big eyes and your sharp intelligence and your habit of fighting back at a challenge . . . You know why I took you up to meet Cathy? I wanted her to see what I'd found, that I'd discovered someone who made me want everything again! And just when I'd acknowledged that, when I thought *you* were beginning to acknowledge it too, you switched yourself off like a light!'

'I'm sorry . . .'

'No, don't be sorry. It was my fault. We'd been so thoroughly in tune just then, so I fell into the stupid error of assuming that if I knew something, you knew it too. How *un*clear can you get?' His expression was rueful, but there was such a light in his face that Bethany felt dazzled by it. 'Little love, tell me it's true *now* and that you're not going to deny it! You're *not* still in love with some idiot who did you harm——'

'No. I'm in love with *you*. I've been trying desperately to tell myself I shouldn't be, that I ought to be disillusioned enough by now not to go on feeling——'

'Don't. Don't you dare try and fight it!'

His lips met hers again with a possessive sweetness that took all her breath away. Her fingers moved up to smooth the crisp blackness of his hair with a quiver of delight that ran down from her fingertips and melted into the passionate joy of his strength holding her, the demanding touch of his mouth. For a long moment there was nothing but this; but when they broke apart again they were both somehow shaken with a joyous laughter.

'Oh, Bethany!'

'Oh, Neil.' She echoed him with a mischievous sparkle in her eyes to match the gleaming, loving amusement in the sapphire eyes looking down at her. 'And I—I didn't even shut the door when I came in!'

'What a shocking example to set with our only woman doctor.' He didn't make the slightest attempt to let her go. 'I knew you'd be trouble . . . This won't get the last days of the accident unit run, will it!'

'How long have we got?'

'To wind everything up? Ten days at the most. They don't mess about when they decided to shut something down. Witness the fact that they've already got a buyer for the house!' He looked up and round with a touch of regret, as if acknowledging Achnabrae's combination of elegance and efficiency. 'It *was* a good idea, in its way. The world's so small with modern transport that it seemed as if it might be a feasible set-up. Ah well—it brought me you, didn't it?'

'You don't think they *really* did all this as a tax dodge?'

'I honestly don't know. I'd rather not be cynical enough to think it was wholly that. There was certainly an element of public relations about it——'

'Mm, Erik said that once.' Bethany evaded the slight threatening gesture he made with one hand and smiled up at him lovingly enough to still any doubts. His response was to let his lips brush hers again, as lightly as a butterfly—but before they could both be caught again into deepening passion he drew back with an obviously forced restraint.

'Listen, my love. This time I'm not going to fall into the trap of thinking you know something because I know it.' He looked down at her with seriousness tingeing the love in his face. 'I'm going back to hospital work, I don't know where yet, but I want you with me. Not just *with* me. I want the lot, marriage, kids— I know it's a lot to ask, but I'm a family man by nature. I also tend towards positively boring fidelity,' he added with a touch of mischief, 'just in case you still insist on having doubts about that——'

'Not boring at all. And——'

'Let me finish. I know it's a lot to ask because for a woman it makes an inevitable break in her career, and there's no way round it. You're too good at your job not to mind that. I just have to make it clear that unfair or not, I want the whole package——Are you interrupting again?'

'I was only going to say, maybe we can both earn enough to afford a nanny? And I'd rather have a broken career than lose out on . . . Oh, *yes,* yes, please, if you're asking, and of course I want the whole package too! And I don't care where we go, either, I just want to be with you!'

Her impassioned, unguarded sincerity set his arms tightening again, and she knew he wouldn't hesitate or ask if she was sure. She was; surer than she had ever been in her life. Every instinct told her so.

And this time there was no need to deny the truth of them, to doubt anything. Bethany lifted her face willingly as Neil's head bent to her again, and her heart sang.

A Mother's Day gift that will last longer than Flowers

MAN OF THE HIGH PLAINS – *Kerry Allyne*
BITTERSWEET HONEYMOON – *Marjorie Lewty*
SHADES OF YESTERDAY – *Leigh Michaels*
PARADISE FOR TWO – *Betty Neels*

Four favourite authors in an exquisite gift pack. There's no better way to show your mother you love her... or you can even treat yourself!

Available from January 1989. Price £5.00

AND THEN HE KISSED HER...

This is the title of our new venture — an audio tape designed to help you become a successful Mills & Boon author!

In the past, those of you who asked us for advice on how to write for Mills & Boon have been supplied with brief printed guidelines. Our new tape expands on these and, by carefully chosen examples, shows you how to make your story come alive. And we think you'll enjoy listening to it.

You can still get the printed guidelines by writing to our Editorial Department. But, if you would like to have the tape, please send a cheque or postal order for £4.95 (which includes VAT and postage) to:

VAT REG. No. 232 4334 96

AND THEN HE KISSED HER...

To: Mills & Boon Reader Service, FREEPOST, P.O. Box 236, Croydon, Surrey CR9 9EL.

Please send me _____ copies of the audio tape. I enclose a cheque/postal order*, crossed and made payable to Mills & Boon Reader Service, for the sum of £ _____ . *Please delete whichever is not applicable.

Signature _____

Name (BLOCK LETTERS) _____

Address _____

_____ Post Code _____

YOU MAY BE MAILED WITH OTHER OFFERS AS A RESULT OF THIS APPLICATION   ED1

IS PASSION A CRIME?

HOT ICE *by Nora Roberts*   £2.95

A reckless, beautiful, wealthy woman and a professional thief. Red hot passion meets cold hard cash and it all adds up to a sizzling novel of romantic suspense.

GAMES *by Irma Walker*   £2.50
(Best selling author of Airforce Wives under the name of Ruth Walker)

Tori Cockran is forced to save her son by the same means that destroyed her marriage and her father — gambling. But first she must prove to the casino boss she loves that she's not a liar and a cheat.

SEASONS OF ENCHANTMENT *by Casey Douglas*   £2.75

Ten years after their broken marriage and the loss of their baby, can Beth and Marsh risk a second chance at love? Or will their differences in background still be a barrier?

All available from February 1989.

W●RLDWIDE

From: Boots, Martins, John Menzies, W H Smith, Woolworths and other paperback stockists.

THREE WOMEN
By Brenda Clarke

'Her work has that rare quality of being difficult to put down'
British Book News

When Joseph Gordon – owner of Gordon's Quality Chocolate factory – married a girl from the factory floor he made it quite plain that her two young nieces were no responsibility of his. Elizabeth and Mary, born to a humbler walk of life, could expect no handouts from their Uncle Joe and their lot was not to be compared with their beautiful pampered cousin, Joe's treasured only daughter, Helen.

But these three girls, Elizabeth and Mary, and the delicate Helen, were to form a bond that all Joe's venom could not break. The passage of two world wars and the years between were to see violent and dramatic changes in their lives and it was Elizabeth, strong, vibrant, working-class and beautiful, who was to be the saviour of the family.

0 552 13260 8

A SCATTERING OF DAISIES
THE DAFFODILS OF NEWENT
BLUEBELL WINDOWS
ROSEMARY FOR REMEMBRANCE
By Susan Sallis

Will Rising had dragged himself from humble beginnings
to his own small tailoring business in Gloucester – and on
the way he'd fallen violently in love with Florence, refined,
delicate, and wanting something better for her children.

March was the eldest girl, the least loved, the plain,
unattractive one who, as the family grew, became more
and more the household drudge. But March, a strange,
intelligent, unhappy child, had inherited some of her
mother's dreams. March Rising was determined to break
out of the round of poverty and hard work, to find wealth,
and love, and happiness.

The story of the Rising girls continues in The Daffodils of
Newent and Bluebell Windows, finally reaching it's
conclusion in Rosemary for Remembrance.

A Scattering of Daisies   0 552 12375 7
The Daffodils of Newent   0 552 12579 2
Bluebell Windows   0 552 12880 5
Rosemary for Remembrance   0 552 13136 9

COPPER KINGDOM
By Iris Gower

The Llewelyns lived in Copperman's Row — a small back-street where the women fought a constant battle against the copper dust from the smelting works. When Mali's mam died there were just two of them left, Malia and her father, sacked from the works for taking time off to nurse his wife. Mali felt she would never hate anyone as much as she hated Sterling Richardson, the young master of the Welsh copper town.

But Sterling had his own problems — bad ones — and not least was the memory of the young green-eyed girl who had spat hatred at him on the day of her mother's death.

COPPER KINGDOM is the first in a sequence of novels set in the South Wales copper industry at the turn of the century.

0 552 12387 0

THE SUMMER OF THE BARSHINSKEYS
By Diane Pearson

'Although the story of the Barshinskeys, which became our story too, stretched over many summers and winters, that golden time of 1902 was when our strange involved relationship began, when our youthful longing for the exotic took a solid and restless hold upon us . . .'

It is at this enchanted moment that *The Summer of the Barshinskeys* begins. A beautifully told, compelling story that moves from a small Kentish village to London, and from war-torn St Petersburg to a Quaker relief unit in the Volgag provinces. It is the unforgettable story of two families, one English, the other Russian, who form a lifetime pattern of friendship, passion, hatred, and love.

'An engrossing saga . . . she evokes rural England at the turn of the century with her sure and skilful touch'
Barbara Taylor Bradford

'The Russian section is reminiscent of Pasternak's *Doctor Zhivago*, horrifying yet hauntingly beautiful'
New York Tribune

0 552 12641 1

RUTH APPLEBY
By Elvi Rhodes

At twelve she stood by her mother's grave on a bleak Yorkshire moor. Life, as the daughter of a Victorian millhand, had never been easy, but now she was mother and housekeeper both to the little family left behind.

As one tribulation after another beset her life, so a longing, a determination grew — to venture out into a new world of independence and adventure, and when the chance came she seized it. America, even on the brink of civil war, was to offer a challenge, that Ruth was ready to accept, and a love, not easy, but glorious and triumphant.

A giant of a book — about a woman who gave herself unstintingly — in love, in war, in the embracing of a new life in a vibrant land.

0 552 12803 1

A SELECTED LIST OF NOVELS AVAILABLE FROM CORGI BOOKS

THE PRICES SHOWN BELOW WERE CORRECT AT THE TIME OF GOING TO PRESS. HOWEVER TRANSWORLD PUBLISHERS RESERVE THE RIGHT TO SHOW NEW RETAIL PRICES ON COVERS WHICH MAY DIFFER FROM THOSE PREVIOUSLY ADVERTISED IN THE TEXT OR ELSEWHERE.

☐	12638 1	**SPINNERS WHARF**	*Iris Gower*	£2.95
☐	12637 3	**PROUD MARY**	*Iris Gower*	£2.95
☐	12387 0	**COPPER KINGDOM**	*Iris Gower*	£2.50
☐	12565 2	**LAST YEAR'S NIGHTINGALE**	*Claire Lorrimer*	£3.50
☐	10584 8	**MAVREEN**	*Claire Lorrimer*	£3.95
☐	11207 0	**TAMARISK**	*Claire Lorrimer*	£2.95
☐	11726 9	**CHANTAL**	*Claire Lorrimer*	£2.95
☐	12182 7	**THE WILDERLING**	*Claire Lorrimer*	£3.50
☐	11959 8	**THE CHATELAINE**	*Claire Lorrimer*	£3.50
☐	10249 0	**BRIDE OF TANCRED**	*Diane Pearson*	£1.95
☐	10375 6	**CSARDAS**	*Diane Pearson*	£3.95
☐	10271 7	**THE MARIGOLD FIELD**	*Diane Pearson*	£2.50
☐	09140 5	**SARAH WHITMAN**	*Diane Pearson*	£2.95
☐	12641 1	**THE SUMMER OF THE BARSHINSKEYS**	*Diane Pearson*	£2.95
☐	12803 1	**RUTH APPLEBY**	*Elvi Rhodes*	£3.95
☐	12367 6	**OPAL**	*Elvi Rhodes*	£2.50
☐	12607 1	**DOCTOR ROSE**	*Elvi Rhodes*	£1.95
☐	11596 7	**FEET IN CHAINS**	*Kate Roberts*	£1.95
☐	11685 8	**THE LIVING SLEEP**	*Kate Roberts*	£2.50
☐	12579 2	**THE DAFFODILS OF NEWENT**	*Susan Sallis*	£2.50
☐	12375 7	**A SCATTERING OF DAISIES**	*Susan Sallis*	£2.75
☐	12880 5	**BLUEBELL WINDOWS**	*Susan Sallis*	£2.50
☐	13136 9	**ROSEMARY FOR REMEMBRANCE**	*Susan Sallis*	£2.95

All Corgi/Bantam Books are available at your bookshop or newsagent, or can be ordered from the following address:
Corgi/Bantam Books,
Cash Sales Department,
P.O. Box 11, Falmouth, Cornwall TR10 9EN

Please send a cheque or postal order (no currency) and allow 60p for postage and packing for the first book plus 25p for the second book and 15p for each additional book ordered up to a maximum charge of £1.90 in UK.

B.F.P.O. customers please allow 60p for the first book, 25p for the second book plus 15p per copy for the next 7 books, thereafter 9p per book.

Overseas customers, including Eire, please allow £1.25 for postage and packing for the first book, 75p for the second book, and 28p for each subsequent title ordered.

NAME (Block Letters) ....

ADDRESS ....

....